The Shell and the Starfish

and other stories

Adele Woodyard

Palm Print Press, Florida

Palm Print Press
P.O. Box 1473
Tarpon Springs, FL 34688
Phone: 727-415-7447
www.palmprintpress.com

ISBN: 978-0-9831069-0-6

Printed in the United States of America

CONTENTS

For Jon, Lee, Jeri, Bonnie, Chris and Scott

Acknowledgements

I'd like to thank the Tarpon Springs Public Library Writers' Group for their most helpful critiques (with apologies for not always following the suggestions). Special thanks go to our leader, author David Edmonds, and such talented writers and artists as Bob, Ann, Georgia, Lee, Sali, Mary, Elizabeth, Mickey, Laura and the late Howard Jones.

Many others have joined the group since then, but these are the ones who re-awakened my imagination and love of writing fiction.

Many thanks to my long-time friend, fellow journalist, one-time editor, sometimes co-author, and first webmaster, Stephen Morrill. I'm ever grateful for his help, generous gift of time, and patience with my lack of computer know-how.

1

THE SHELL AND THE STARFISH

Damn it, Casey thought blinking back angry tears, I never should have signed up for this Caribbean trip. The chance to flee the remnants of a failed marriage, to literally sail into the sunset, was a lure she'd been unable to resist. Only now the hot tropical sun, a beach lapped by a gentle aquamarine sea, the mask and fins that dangled from her fingers, all reminded her of David in a series of flashbacks she was desperate to forget.

A dinghy from one of the four chartered sailboats scraped ashore, the sound grating on nerves already rubbed raw by the sands of memory. Casey gritted her teeth as the boat's laughing, chattering cargo spilled onto the beach.

"Oh, look at the sand castle," one woman said. "Did you build it?"

Casey looked behind her. Thick, slanted walls supported turrets decorated with bits of coral, scraps of shells. She and David had built such a castle on a beach in the Virgin Islands on their honeymoon. "Our dream house," David had said, sculpting the sand into shape. That overnight became a crumbling remnant eaten away by the tide.

Her mouth twisted into a bitter grimace. "I didn't even know it was there."

One eyebrow raised on the woman's round, sunburned face. With a shrug, she pulled a mask over her head and turned away. Casey's eyes sought the water.

A scatter of miniature periscopes glided over the shallow reefs of the Tobago Cays. Knee-deep amid exposed rocks a gray haired man scrabbled beneath the surface with gloved hands. Sails furled, their boats bobbed at anchor, masts silhouetted against a cloudless, china-blue sky. Her mind framed the beauty of the scene, longed to capture its serenity.

"Peaceful, isn't it."

Startled, Casey turned her head. Ron Stewart, one of the six people assigned to her boat, smiled down at her. Tanned, blond and blue eyed he was a good looking man despite a scarred chest and slightly deformed right hand. She guessed he was in his late thirties. "I wish some of that peace would rub off on me," she said, thinking *if only everything could be the way it was…*

He nodded. "Took me a long time to stop wishing. To accept the fact you can't get back what you've lost."

She stared up at him, afraid he'd read her mind. At her

questioning look Ron pointed toward the scar that ran in a jagged line below the sternum. "My wife and son were killed in the wreck." His voice held no emotion. But his gaze, fastened on some distant scene only he could see, held so much pain it made her cringe.

"How—awful," Casey whispered. *Why are you telling me this?* The desire to reach out and hold him, comfort him, grappled with a sudden anger at him for making her feel that way. The automatic "I'm so sorry" further twisted her emotions into a tighter knot.

"Thank God it was the other guy's fault." Ron shook his head. "Crazy, isn't it? I mean, being thankful for something like that. But having someone else to blame—maybe that's what helped me to survive." He looked away.

Shaken, Casey stared at her feet. Curled her toes in the sand as she thought of the way Ron was on the boat. Always pleasant. Helpful. A good sailor who did his part but never said much. One of the women described it as a wall between himself and everyone else. Only now—she felt as it the shield was ripped, the wall sprung a leak. She shifted her weight, resenting his confession as if he'd broken an unwritten law.

"I'm sorry," he said. "I shouldn't have dumped this—it was just…" his gesture swept their surroundings, "we used to…"

"I know." With a sigh Casey admitted , "I have the same trouble."

The silence grew oppressive. An uneasy glance from the corner of her eye ran headlong into his. "You want to snorkel?"

Casey flashed him a grateful smile. As they walked across the sand, Ron asked "How long have you been divorced ?"

"Almost a year." *Long enough to get over it, to get on with my life.*

"Any kids?"

"Fortunately no."

Would you have left me David, if there was a child? I wanted one, remember? A boy with your brown eyes that sparkle so when you laugh, and turn so fierce when you're angry. Or maybe a girl with my curly hair you said was like fire...

She stumbled.

"Hey." Ron caught her by the arm. "You okay?"

She nodded, her smile crooked. "I was just..." *What? Mourning a child that never was, a marriage that ended? How can it mean anything to a man who's had both ripped from his arms?*

Casey shook her head. Muttered, "It's nothing."

Slipping on mask and fins they entered the water to glide over an underwater forest of golden coral heads, waving lavender sea fans, and thick-branched elkhorn. Her eyes tried to follow the schools of fish that darted amongst them, fascinated by their varied shapes and brilliant colors. Vaguely conscious of a pair of legs moving nearby.

On their honeymoon she and David would snorkel side by side, like this. Frequently they'd touch, or reach for the other's arm if one happened to see something out of the ordinary. As she was doing now…

Only no one was there. She lifted her head above water. Ron must have swam away. An unexpected surge of loneliness swept through her, leaving her feeling empty. Memory of those endless nights after David left rippled upwards like disturbed grains of sand. Nights when she prowled through the house unable to sleep. Unwilling to return to a singles bed. But that was the past. She'd grown used to living alone, even liked it that way. Didn't she?

The gray-haired man she knew was a marine biologist, was still grubbing in the shallows. A sudden need for human contact urged Casey to paddle to him. "Hi, Bert," she said. "Find anything worth keeping?"

Without a word he held out a shell for her to examine. Deep red globules were staggered around the irregular calcified surface like so many drops of blood.

"You won't see many of these," Bert said, identifying it in the original and barely pronounceable Latin. A professor to the core, she thought but murmured, "Very interesting

"Having a good time?"

"Great," she lied, taken aback by the look of appraisal in his eyes.

Bert gave a brief nod and bent to study the bottom beneath their feet. His gloved hand plunged into the water to surface with a starfish. "This one's called a brittle star," he said and placed it in her hand.

Spiny red tentacles curled around her fingers. Its mouth worked its way along her palm. Startled, Casey grasped one of its arms only to have it break off in her hand. "Oh no," she cried, as the creature fell into the sea.

"Don't worry about it," Bert said. "It'll grow another. Did you notice that three of the five rays were longer than the others?" She shook her head. "The shorter ones were lost and re-grown." When he added "Shame we humans can only replace our lost limbs from within," Casey could almost read "get the message?" in his eyes.

She blinked, unable to respond. He shrugged and glanced at his watch. "Ah, close to happy hour, I see. Time to get back to the boat. You coming?"

"Not yet." Replacing the mask, she slid back into deeper water. What was he trying to tell her? And why? So he knew she was divorced. But losing a mate was hardly the same as losing an arm. Or was it?

Casey frowned. She and David *had* grown together, became intertwined through the day to day routine of marriage. They'd depended on each other to be in the next room, to share the same bed. To walk off, yet always come back. Only this time he hadn't come back. She grimaced. Maybe that was like losing an arm, after all.

No, she thought, it's not a good analogy, and slapped the water with a fin. A starfish feels no pain. We hurt when we lose someone we love. Are afraid it'll happen again. Casey lifted her head, her eyes searching for Ron. *The agony that he must have gone though...no wonder he'd built a wall around himself...*

And you, Casey. Aren't you afraid to grow another arm?

The little voice echoed in her brain, an unwanted intrusion. She tried to swim away from it, but the parade of images it spawned would not stop.

Sitting alone on the deck under the stars, while her shipmates laughed over a board game in the cabin below. Seeking a corner in whatever boat hosted a party. Straggling behind the group when they explored a town on shore. Like Ron she tried to exclude herself from the others. Casey inwardly recoiled. The picture it drew was of a woman drowning in self-pity.

The islet before her was deserted. She pulled off her fins and waded ashore. Behind her a loaded dinghy was heading back to a boat. Another was already tied by its painter. Running her fingers through wet curls, she rounded the point of the beach. A heap of Queen conch shells was piled against the rocky hillside. Casey picked out one whose translucent pink fan curved into a deep rose whorl. At the sound of an approaching motor, she lifted her head.

"It's getting late," Ron said, as he beached the dinghy. "I've been sent to collect the strays." His glance fell on the shell cradled in her arms. "Planning to take it with you?"

Nodding, she pointed to the small hole where the natives had jerked out the meat. "Maybe this will remind me that growing a hard shell can't protect me from being hurt."

For what seemed an endless moment his eyes bored into hers. Then he walked over to the pile of shells and chose one. He picked it up and, without saying a word, turned and held out his hand.

She hesitated, unsure of what he wanted. At his smile she placed a tentative hand in his. Ron drew her to him, close enough to feel the warmth of his body, to imagine the taste of its salt. "Thank you," he said. Eyes still fastened to hers, he brought her fingers to his lips. The kiss was so gentle it made no sound yet later, Casey would swear she heard the chip of mortar and the muffled crash of falling bricks.

Honorable Mention: *Writer's Digest* Short Story Contest, 1992

2

THE STORM

The fishing pier at Bayport is an unsteady wooden addition to the rock-walled parabola of land. Harry Dawson leans his bulk against the waist-high railing and peers below him. Fed by inland springs the water is black with hidden weeds and faintly salty, as it races to the waiting Gulf of Mexico.

"Tide's sure going out strong," he says, pulling just hard enough on the Dacron line looped around his hand to take up the slack.

The man beside him grunts in agreement. He is taller than Harry, with sandy hair and a lean, passive face. Propping his spinning rod between elbow and forearm, he lights a cigarette. Harry involuntarily reaches for the pocket of his tattered plaid shirt, remembers he gave up smoking, and hitches up dirty khaki pants instead. What difference does it make anymore? He is seventy-seven years old and still healthy as a horse. For what? He glares back at Myrt who sits on the unpainted dock, her feet resting on the catwalk. She is .staring vacantly into space. He turns away, half glad, half annoyed that she is not paying any attention to him. After fifty-eight years there is very little left to say

"Hey Daddy," look at that sky." A stocky, tow-headed boy tugs at the other man's arm, round blue eyes alight with anticipation as he points overhead. "Is the hurricane coming now?"

Glancing up, Harry can see the heavens seemingly split in two. Darkening clouds tumble on one side, while the other still reflects the quiet sheen of the Gulf. A quickening breeze rustles the mangroves that rise in twisted clumps above the sawgrass flats.

"Not yet, son," the man says. "These are outriders. The hurricane's still a long ways away."

Harry snorts. "Looks like a li'l ole thunderstorm to me. There's a lot of 'em this time of year."

The man's mouth tightens. "Maybe so, but there's a big one headin' this way. Or haven't you heard?"

"Yeah, sure. But what's the big deal? Sometimes I think Florida 's the safest place to be. Why I remember back in West Virginia—'61 it was—we had a real humdinger. The rains poured off them mountains into little streams which flooded out Charleston. That's the state capital. Anyways, my boys—I have—had four," he corrects himself, thinking it's still hard to get used to, Bert dying of a heart attack like that when he was only forty-one.

"A girl too, but that's no matter to my story . Was no place for womenfolk. Anyways me and my boys and some others went down to help out. Water up to our necks. Found an ole woman floatin' on a mattress, clear up under her roof. She didn't have much space left."

"Geez," the boy breathed.

"You'd think the house would've gone with that much water," the man says, eyes narrow with suspicion.

"Over a thousand of 'em did. But not that one." Harry smiles at the boy's expectant face. "After the water went down everything was covered with mud. 'Specially the south part where the quarters were. It being low and all. In some spots it was still waist deep. And stink! Boy, what a mess. A lot of folks died in that storm."

He looks away, suddenly uncomfortable with the surge of memory he had sworn to forget. *Stumbling over an obstacle, the sucking sound as he pulled it free. The body of a child, a boy maybe five at the outside, so covered with mud he couldn't tell if the kid was white or black.* As if it mattered.

Clutching his son by the arm the man says, "Come on, Jimmy. Your mom's waitin' on us," and turns to go.

Harry watches them walk toward a long concrete picnic table laden with food, crowded with people. Men lounge around the fireplace drinking beer while a self-appointed chef dishes up hamburgers to an assembly line of paper plates. Children tumble on the grass, clamber over empty tables, a small dog yapping at their heels. One boy has found a spigot on a standing pipe and turned it on, jamming his finger across the spout so it sprays everyone within reach. Women scold him amid the shrieks, and herd their offspring back to the common trough. The babble of voices fills the air without words.

It makes no difference: Harry can repeat every phrase of the familiar theme. Only the setting is altered. Memory replaces the clustered shelters on concrete slabs with long planks laid on sawbucks, the backdrop of tangled bayhead with mountain ash and laurel, the muddy, still-water canal with an ice cold, rockbound stream. His eyes sweep this flat, alien land searching for the mountains that are not there, and he wonders why they had ever come.

When he retired his friends had slapped him on the back, crying "You lucky dog. Nothing to do all day but lay around and fish," and winking, "Hey, Harry, how about them bathin' beauties," and "Boy, what a life." Florida. Saved and scrimped for over the long, hard years. Dream come true. He had laughed and kidded with them, rubbing their workworn faces in the sands of his freedom while, even then, the emptiness inside him had grown bigger and bigger. If his friends could only see him now. Nothing to do but fish. Exactly.

A gust of wind tugs at his thinning white hair and he raises his eyes. Above him the clouds are gathering for a massive frontal assault. Already a small vanguard has pierced the pale perimeter of the western sky. A growing rumble warns of approaching artillery. Rain, damn you, he thinks. Flood this whole stinkin' state…

Bending, he hauls in his line. The four sided trap contains seaweed, a frayed hunk of mullet, and two medium-sized crabs. Harry scowls at them, loathing the hard, speckled carapace, the pinching blue claws. Damn crabs. "If I never eat another bit of seafood," he mutters under his breath, "I'll die happy."

He spreads the trap, shaking the crabs loose into a bushel basket. They'll be good for a free drink at "Zelma's" anyway. It isn't a bad arrangement he and Myrt have with the hole-in-the-wall restaurant, what with the limits of Social Security. Booze and an occasional meal in exchange for fresh fish. The only problem is, Zelma specializes in seafood and he can never seem to drink enough.

Harry straightens to rest his arms on the railing. The water stretches before him, a silver sheet of glass flowing into silver clouds without a break to mark the horizon. Several black posts stud the channel like so many cloves. Two fishing boats thread their way home, stark silhouettes leaving barely a ripple. Dusk. Earth, sky and water suspended in a moment of silence. He holds his breath, waiting for a peace that will not come.

He senses a presence beside him, knows without looking that it is Myrt. "I'm going to trade the trailer for a boat," he says.

A deep growl of thunder breaks the stillness. "Why, Harry?" she asks. "It won't stop the tide from going out."

He stares down at his hands, clenched now over the railing. They are broad, with blunt, callused fingers, the knuckles lined in the indelible ink of coal. Hands that had once been of use. Hands that now smell of decaying fish. *Why did you have to say that for?*

Harry raises his head to look at her. *My God, but she is old.* Flaccid white flesh splaying in a million tiny wrinkles. Myopic brown eyes that squint behind thick glasses. He can see bits of scalp peeking through hair yellowed with age. Their eyes lock and hold for an endless moment, then she turns and walks to the end of the dock. Must have seen herself in my glasses, he thinks, suddenly grateful he has not seen his reflection in hers.

The uneven boards tremble beneath his feet and he looks around. A young couple is coming toward him, arms about each other's waist. The girl is a pretty little thing, good figure. She smiles and Harry pulls himself erect.

"Looks like we're in for a real blow," the youth says, squinting at the sky. Mouse colored hair brushes his collar, a thin line of down shades his upper lip.

"I hate storms, especially hurricanes," the girl says with a shiver. But her large dark eyes gleam with excitement.

"Yep, they can be bad," Harry agrees. He is conscious of needing a haircut as he tilts back his head. The menacing clouds have breached the invisible wall. They roll across the sky, turning the water to indigo, and behind them he can hear the muffled drumming of approaching rain.

"I remember back in West Virginia," he begins, but two fat drops of water splatter against his face, and he knows he will not finish.

Awarded First place, 1989. Published *The WordSmith*, 1990, *Time Out Tampa Bay*, 1993.

3

THE SISTER

The dinner was not going well. Rebecca eyed the flower-filled bowl that matched the Waterford crystal; silently admired the cutwork cloth she had bought in Bermuda last summer. That time she'd talked George into taking a cruise. *Why if it wasn't for her he'd never get out of the house. Except to work.* Only now—the lump in her throat tasted sour. The meal may have been cooked to perfection, but her stomach was in rebellion. Eyes downcast, she picked at the food on her plate, reluctant to face the source of the conflict.

She didn't need to look, to know the woman who sat opposite her had dark hair that brushed her shoulders, and brown eyes brimming with laughter. High cheekbones. A generous mouth with teeth so white and even, Rebecca was sure they were all capped. And that figure—she glowered at the pink and blue flowers, the gold band rimming her plate, hating her own too-long face, the too-big teeth. All too aware that behind her back, co-workers--even those she supervised-- called her "Horse". And did the woman have to look so young? The bile rose with her resentment at being made to feel like a frumpy old lady when she, Rebecca, was only 46.

"George tells me you two are very close. That you practically raised him," the woman whose name was Sally, said.

"I did what I could," Rebecca muttered to the meat on her plate. It was roast beef medium rare, the way George liked it…The glance she flicked at her brother wavered between fear and irritation. *Did he also tell her how Mom died in a car wreck? Because she was drunk?*

George sat between them at the head of the table, a fatuous grin on his face. *Men in love look so witless.* Startled, Rebecca shrank from the instinctive thought, unwilling to acknowledge the meaning behind his stupid, senseless smile.

"I have two brothers," Sally said. "One younger, one older. They can be great to have around. Sometimes. When they're not being a pain in the butt." She gave an indulgent laugh, looked to Rebecca for confirmation. Rebecca responded with a grudging, thin-lipped smile.

"Sally is an actress," George said.

"Would be," she corrected him.

"Are," he insisted, turning to Rebecca. "You should have seen her Kate, sis, in *The Taming of the Shrew*. It was the best I've seen."

"Oh? When was that? I don't remember our…"

"It was about six months ago," Sally said. "First Act" put it on. In fact that's how George and I met. At the audition."

Icy fingers reached for her heart as Rebecca looked from one to the other. It was the same sensation she'd felt when she had learned the "friend" George was bringing to dinner was a woman. "Audition?"

Red-faced, George avoided eye contact. "Okay, so I tried out. I was going to tell you, only I didn't get a part." Flush deepening, he confessed, "I was so bad they wouldn't even let me be an extra."

Sally squeezed his hand. "A lot of people get stage fright. Besides, you make a great stagehand."

"George is too sensitive, too retiring to be on stage," Rebecca said, wondering when did he ever get the idea of being an actor? "He wanted to be an artist once, too. But there's no money in that, either."

Sally looked up at him, eyes wide. "An artist? Really? I know you're talented—I've seen some of your work as a draftsman, but…"

Rebecca frowned. "He could have been an engineer. You do know he has a daughter to support?"

"Of course." Sally's voice was beginning to slip on a coat of frost. "You have any children?"

"I'm an office manager," Rebecca said, refusing to admit she'd never married. "Supervise seven employees. It's a small company."

The question had uncovered an empty pit. Her eyes traveled around the sunlit room in a familiar if futile effort to fill the void. Pink and mauve blossoms bloomed on upholstered furniture surrounded by ficus trees, palms and hanging plants. Excitable finches twittered in a bamboo cage. A fat brass frog squatted by sliding glass doors that opened onto a balcony. Tall downtown buildings framed the lone sailboat on the narrow bay. It was an ever-changing picture she never tired of viewing. To her its price tag was the symbol of her success, her self-worth as a woman.

"You do have a lovely place," Sally said.

Rebecca's gaze slid past her to rest on her brother. "Coffee now or later?" she asked.

****

Rebecca had a splitting headache. She added two more aspirin to those she had taken earlier, grateful that it was a holiday and she did not have to go to work. Clean laundry was heaped high on her bed. She began to sort and fold the pieces into two piles, hers to the left, George's boxer shorts, T-shirts, handkerchiefs and socks to the right. Twice a week she picked up his laundry, dirty clothes one day, sheets and towels the next, for her stacked washer/dryer combination could only hold small loads.

"You shouldn't be doing this," George kept saying until her repeated assurances it was "no problem" finally shut him up. He just doesn't understand, she thought, rolling up a pair of his socks. Doing his laundry, having him to dinner every Sunday since his divorce, was nothing compared to all the years she had taken care of him as a little boy. George barely remembered the father who died when he was four and she was ten. How she'd become his second mother when their mom had to go to work...The years when she'd been needed.

Her pounding head made her eyes squint. Forced her to remember last night's unanswered phone calls. *Had George even made it home? If there was an accident, surely she'd have heard by now--it was almost noon.* Rebecca gritted her teeth and kept folding the clothes, unwilling to think of another reason he had not returned her call.

After dividing her things among the dresser drawers, Rebecca placed George's piles into a plastic bag and picked up her keys. There was one for his house on her keychain, just as he had one for her condo. It had been that way even when he was married. Setting the bag on the passenger seat of her car, she closed her door and turned the ignition key,

George still lived in the modest frame house they had grown up in and where he had brought his bride. A trifle shabby now, crumbling around the edges like a stale cake, the house sat on an oak shaded street less than a mile away. If it wasn't for the laundry—and the pride she felt in driving her red sports car—she could have walked.

Rebecca found him in the kitchen making a sandwich and wearing an expression of dreamy contentment. Her lips pursed as she recognized the look of a man who has spent the night wrapped in a blanket of loving sex. The image was so unsettling, she refused his offer of food and drink.

George popped the top of his beer. Sliding onto a chair at the scarred maple topped table, he asked "Well, sis, what do you think of Sally?"

Rebecca studied their initials he had carved in the table top long ago. The "R S" and "G S" were black with an accumulation of imbedded dirt. "She seems like a nice woman," she finally admitted. "But isn't she a little—young?"

He grinned. "Fooled you too, huh? Believe it or not, Sally's 32."

Eight years younger than he. Frowning, she traced their initials with one finger. "A 32 year old actress who's still doing little theatre? How does she live?"

"Modeling. Commercials. She does okay." George paused in taking a bite of the sandwich, cocked a quizzical eyebrow. "What are you getting at anyway?"

"You may not be wealthy but you make good money. A woman with such a nebulous income…" Rebecca halted, stunned into silence by the sudden flush of anger on his face. George, who had never been one for confrontation, who would rather run away if he couldn't hold it in, looked ready to explode. "I—I just mean she'll want to get m-m-married." To her relief, the rage leaked from his face as if from a pin-pricked balloon when she added the words "if she loves you."

"You really think so?"

"That's what usually happens." The confidence that she was riding on the right track faltered on a sudden curve. "But you've been against marrying again ever since Alma left." Her eyes sought his as she asked, "Are you changing your mind?"

George gave her a blank stare. Swallowing a smile, Rebecca rose to her feet. "Sally is a good woman," she said. "A nice person like her doesn't deserve to be hurt. And she will be if you continue to string her along." She turned to leave, oblivious to the fact her brother was too lost in thought to say goodbye.

Rebecca was putting the final touches to the following Sunday's dinner table when George walked in. She kissed him on the cheek. "Where's Sally? I thought she was coming with you."

He shook his head. "She—I think maybe we're through."

It was then she noticed the shadows under his eyes. The dejected slump of his shoulders. "Oh George, I'm so sorry," she said, dropping her gaze to conceal her delight. Giving his arm a gentle squeeze, Rebecca asked, "What happened? Or don't you want to talk about it."

He collapsed into a chair with a long drawn-out sigh of self-pity. "What does it matter? It's all my fault…"

"What do you mean, your fault?" Taking a stand behind him Rebecca began to knead his shoulders and the nape of his neck. His hair, once brown like hers but tightly curled, was threaded with gray strands resembling kinky wire. She could see a spot beginning to bald on the crown.

"You're always blaming yourself for no reason," she said. "This is no more your fault than when Alma walked out."

"I made the mistake when I asked her to marry me."

Marry? Rebecca gripped the back of the chair as the blood drained from her face. When George tried to look at her she put her hands back on his neck, forcing it forward and resumed the massage.

"I thought over what you said." His voice was muffled. "About her being hurt and all, and then it hit me. I really was in love with her. Didn't want to lose her." His laugh was short, rueful, surprised. "Only it turned out Sally likes it just the way we were." Rebecca winced as he muttered, "…no more than a friendly fuck."

"But you've been telling me right along you'd never get married again."

"And I meant it. It hurt like hell when Alma left. I'd tried so hard—at least I thought I was a good husband. A good father, and then—only it's been over two years now, sis. I get lonely. You should understand that, better than anyone."

Rebecca could feel the ice closing in, not with fingers this time but in a solid block that filled her chest, squeezing her breath.

"In fact," George went on, "Sally bawled me out. About my taking so much of your time when you could be giving it to a man you could marry. Hell, I never thought—never dreamed-- Can you ever forgive me?"

Her response was a strangled "erk".

Rising to his feet he turned and placed his hands on her shoulders. "Sally told me the only way I can thank you enough is to say, get on with your life."

"But—but…"

George shook his head, gave her a quick hug. "No buts. From now on it's no more laundry. Fewer Sunday dinners. And forget all those other treats you keep bringing me. Hear?"

The ice had been spreading throughout her body. Rebecca stared at him, too numb to think. The one certainty she could grasp was that the child she once cared for was gone. Facing her was a man, a stranger, and she was not sure she liked him at all.

4

I MARRIED MY PARENTS

They looked very small. The side of the cruise ship loomed above me, gleaming so white in the Florida sun, I had to squint to see them. Laughing and waving, they leaned over the ship's railing, my father's dark head touched with gray, Mom's still blonde. Like mine. But I have his eyes, a soft brown the color of cocoa, turning into liquid now with my tears.

"You okay?"

I blinked them away. The man beside me was tall, with thick sandy hair, long, hard muscles and shoulders wide enough to snuggle against.

"Oh Kevin," I said, giving myself a hug, "I couldn't be happier."

We were jostled by the crowd that waved good-bye and yelled things like "bon voyage" and "cheerio" as the big ship thrust itself away from the wharf. Water boiled and foamed at bow and stern, to subside into a rippling stream of sun-streaked blue. Multi-colored flags snapped overhead.

I watched it glide down the channel, with a whispered "Happy honeymoon" to a mother and father I hadn't even met until a few short months ago. Being a notary public, as well as their daughter, I'd just performed their marriage ceremony 23 years late.

The picture of them standing before me repeated itself, an endless loop in my mind. She, radiant in a rose silk suit. He, standing proud in dark suit and tie. Their attendants, Betty and Art...

"Lisa. Earth calling Lisa. Come in, come in, wherever you are," interrupted my reverie.

Kevin's grey-green eyes crinkled at the corners. "I think," he said, "we'd better go."

Surprised, I glanced around us. The pier was deserted. Seagulls, that had swirled above the ship, now perched on pilings or half-heartedly pecked through the flotsam at the water's edge. A sudden breeze swooshed across the concrete like a damp mop. I shivered. "What time is it?"

He peered at his watch. "Almost five o'clock."

"Why didn't you say something?"

"You were in another world. And from the look on your face, I wasn't about to spoil the trip."

"Can you blame me? For the first time in my life, I feel complete. Thanks to you."

"What are you talking about? I didn't do anything."

I stared up at him, remembering how he'd stood stiffly apart at the ceremony, as if he didn't belong. Wondering why his voice had an angry edge.

"You only found my mother. Isn't that enough?"

Kevin shrugged. "Glad to be of help," he muttered, steering me to his car.

I watched him slide behind the wheel, silently willing him to open his arms, his heart to me. As I've done since the day we met almost ten months ago. Considering there's seventy-five lawyers and three times as many support people in the law firm we both work for, it was close to a miracle it happened at all. If I hadn't joined the rush of "throwaways" looking for their biological parents and drawn a blank, I doubt if we'd have ever gotten together.

Fortunately much of his job is in research. I found him amid the files of former cases, dusty statutes, and forgotten laws. When we introduced ourselves, I felt the spark was immediate and mutual. Once again I wondered if it was only my imagination. If it was all one-sided. My side.

"I never dreamed that finding my mother would lead to my father too, " I said, unwilling to let it go. "It's like you have all six numbers in Lotto, when you thought you had only three."

"You didn't tell me how that happened."

You never asked me, I thought. But once past the initial digging, everything had come together so quickly, as if time was running out—"It was my father who came to her." Like Prince Charming, the knight on a white horse, Romeo and Juliet all rolled into one. The wonder at the fairy tale ending echoed in my voice.

"He had married," I went on, "they both had, and after his wife died—she, my mother, was divorced. But you know that, and..." I turned to the window, tried to swallow the lump that pushed against my throat. "He never knew about me," I said, and burst into tears.

"Hey, don't. Don't cry. Please."

We'd come to a stop. Embarrassed, I looked up, struggling for control. Above us lights shone in some of the windows in the apartment building where I lived. "I'm sorry," I muttered, and rummaged in my purse for a tissue.

He opened my door. "Feel better?"

I nodded. Blew my nose. "They'd never stopped loving each other," I said, stepping out of the car. "Can you believe that? After all those years apart."

"Well—yeah. I guess it could happen."

"I say it calls for a celebration." My hand rested on the sleeve of his jacket. "Will you join me for another toast?"

He hesitated. Glanced down at my hand. "Ah, why not?" and followed me into my apartment.

Dirty glasses, the remains of a wedding cake were still on the table. With a "Make yourself comfortable," I began to pick up what my hands could hold.

Kevin lifted the cake. "I'd rather help."

The kitchen in my one bedroom apartment is smaller than most walk-in closets. It was hard to keep from bumping into each other. I hurriedly found clean glasses, handed him the champagne to uncork, too aware of his maleness. At least the apartment has a balcony. It was a relief to step outside. Until I was faced with the best way to phrase a toast to "love".

Kevin solved that dilemma with a cliched "Cheers." We touched glasses, took the obligatory sip, as a dying sun unfolded a rosy fan across the sky. His question, "How come your father didn't know she was pregnant?" broke the silence. .

"When they met and fell in love, she was barely sixteen. He was in college. In another state. Mom told me her parents sent her to a place for unwed mothers and insisted she give me up for adoption. She had to promise never to see me, or my father again." I frowned. Took a deep swallow. "These people were -- are--my grandparents. I hope I never meet them."

"I can see why they did what they did. She was just a kid herself. You haven't had it so bad, have you?"

I tried to imagine what my life would have been like if she'd kept me, but a clear picture wouldn't come together. I shook my head.

"Maybe you even have some half-brothers and sisters."

My laugh sounded weak. "From what Mom told me, I have one of each." Between earlier toasts and the emotional day, the champagne is making me woozy. "After being an only child for so long, it's hard to imagine a ready-made family."

"With two sets of parents. How did the Williams take it when you first told them you wanted to find your birth mother?"

I recalled the look on Mom—Betty's face, when I brought it up. Her expression when she and my biological mother actually met. Me denying her pain with a "women always cry at weddings," at her tears today.

"She never tried to hide the fact I was adopted," I said. "In fact she even told me someday I might want to look for my real mother and, if I did, they wouldn't stand in the way."

Suddenly the love built through all my growing up years came at me with the force of a hatchet. It chunked off bits and pieces of memories: birthday cakes and Christmas trees; a Shetland pony; summers at the beach; camp where I cried myself to sleep, and learned to make friends. The long walks with Dad—Art, and long talks with Mom—Betty. I closed my eyes tight. *How could I call them by their names now when they've been Mom and Dad for as long as I've lived?*

I opened my eyes to find Kevin watching my face. I glared at him, angry at myself. "When I asked you how to find my parents, you wanted to know why."

"So, why did you? You admitted you had a good life, that your adopted parents would do anything for you. So what if you weren't of their blood. What difference should that make to you now, an adult, when it made no difference to them? To them you were their child."

"But I'm not. And that's the reason. How would you know what that's like, wondering who your real parents are, if you look like your mother, or maybe your dad. What did he do for a living? Where, and how, did they live? *Why did she give me up?*" The tears threatened to overflow in an irreversible flood, and I forced them back. "You wouldn't—couldn't, know what it's like."

All expression drained from Kevin's face. "You're right," he admitted. "I wouldn't know. Both my parents died in an auto accident when I was ten years old."

Only the swish of a passing car broke the shocked silence. I stared at him, then at my feet. Finally I whispered, "Oh God, Kevin, I'm so sorry."

He poured himself a drink, and filled my glass. "I'm sorry too," he said, "for being jealous."

"Jealous?"

"Or resentful. Probably both. You see, after I lost my folks, I was put in a foster home. Homes—that should be plural. There were six of them before I was old enough to be on my own. So when you waltzed in trying to find someone I could never have again, especially when you already had it all—well…" Kevin shrugged and drained his glass.

The pieces began to fall into place. The way he held himself, as if afraid of touching, and being touched. He'd lost those he loved when still young enough to be vulnerable. Old enough to remember. No wonder he'd shied away from me.

And yet—"If you felt so strongly, why did you help me? You did more than tell me where and how to look for information. You went and found my mother yourself. Why did you go to all that trouble?"

"Because I knew I was being stupid." His eyes looked into mine and I saw I'd been right the first time we'd met. The feeling between us was not one-sided after all. It circled around us, growing ever smaller, pushing us together—I blinked, surprised to find we hadn't moved at all.

One hand lifted my chin. "Tell me," he half-whispered, "I'm not being stupid now."

The only way I could answer him was to return his kiss. And the circle that tightened around me was the one drawn by his arms.

5

SONG OF THE FAMILY

I stared at the two gold rings behind the glass, feeling trapped in a dirty pocket of a recessed doorway. "Why do you want to get married?"

"Because I love you."

Surprise and hurt echoed in his voice, were mirrored in eyes the color of hazelnuts. My heart twisted until tears crowded my throat. "And I love you," I said "but marriage—that's a big step. I've got to have time, Greg. To think."

"Yeah. I understand." He shrugged as if it didn't matter, but I knew we both felt miserable. I eased past him, not making contact. He kept his eyes on a man's watch in the window. It had a gold mesh band and no numerals.

I plunged into the crowd without looking back. The city pummeled me from all sides. Bodies shoved, jabbed, sweated. Dirt filtered through the Manhattan sky, clogging pores, burning eyes. The subway was packed, its stations already drawing a stream of unwashed homeless seeking to escape the cold October night.

I hung onto a strap, jammed between a woman built like a tank and a man who reeked of garlic. In my imagination Greg's face was etched on the dirty window; curly dark hair, strong nose, sensitive mouth, his eyes flecked with wistful dreams. I remembered when we'd met a year ago, courtesy of our mutual employer. How we'd laughed when we discovered the country yokels hiding behind a thin veneer of New York City sophistication. Greg came from a sleepy town in Ohio. I'm from the hills of eastern Pennsylvania where main street stores string a necklace worn by farmers. My parents never understood why I left.

My apartment was filled with shadows, yet strangely empty. I circled the narrow living room, the tiny bedroom barely large enough for bed and bureau, imagining Greg sharing it with me. His clothes in my closet, my dresser. Shaving equipment in the bathroom. His face across the table, every day. *Isn't that what I want? Or am I afraid he'll smother who I am as he invades my space?*

The air felt so stuffy I opened a window. Vaporous yellow lights had begun to shine through the murky gray haze. Above the swish-swish of tires, a boom box bouncing heavy metal off the walls, I heard a drawn-out "Bobbee—Bobbie. Supper!" and was turned into a kid again. It was time to go home.

****

Hopeville is a town surrounded by woods and farms built on the rocky backs of abandoned coal mines. I drove down the main artery past my father's hardware store, now closed for the night. At the edge of Main Street I turned right and began to climb. The house, painted the nauseating color of Gulden's mustard, sat atop a high terrace. Through the back door glass I could see my mother, hunched over a metal table, writing on a tablet. Her hair, once smooth and dark like mine, had been tortured into frizzy curls. It reminded me of a wire brush clotted with Dutch Cleanser. Her cheeks were too plump to show wrinkles, yet she looked older than I remembered. It upset me.

She jumped at my knock, one hand flying to her breast.

"It's me. Mom. Kathy."

A hug, a nervous spate of words greeted me at the door. "I didn't hear you drive in, you scared me half out of my wits. So late—you didn't call or anything, so I wasn't expecting—what a nice surprise, dear." Holding me at arm's length, she peered into my face. "Are you all right?"

"Of course I'm all right."

"Well, it being Friday and all—"

"So I came home." I pulled away. "How's Dad?"

"Sleeping." She trailed after me as I headed for the refrigerator, her empty hands reaching, aimless. "Hungry? Let me fix you something."

"Just thirsty," I said, pulling out a can of soda past plastic bowls with colored lids. "I ate on the road."

She resumed her seat and pushed at the papers before her with pudgy fingers. "I was just writing a letter to Robbie."

"How's he doing?"

"Fine." The response was automatic; the frown that creased her forehead belied the word. "Oh, I don't know. His grades—"

"I thought he'd made them up." I recalled the shock at the end of spring term. Rob, an honor roll student all through school, had been placed on academic probation. But then Penn State is a far cry from Hopeville High.

She nodded, then said, "Your father blames the professors. Says they give the kids wrong ideas."

"Oh, Mom, for heaven's sake." I wanted to shout, *how would he know?* He never went to college. None of us did. I had a year of secretarial school. Frank's an auto mechanic. If Rob hadn't won a football scholarship, he wouldn't have made it either. They pay more for sports than brains.

She finally asked, "How's Greg?"

"Fine." *If only she knew.* I recalled the newspaper clippings of former classmates' weddings, baby showers and births, she kept tucking into my letters. I didn't want to talk about it. Kissing her goodnight, I headed for my room.

Before climbing the stairs, I stopped in the living room where photos of our family were tacked to one wall. Me, as a cheerleader. Frank, the Eagle Scout. Robbie in his football uniform, leaping for a pass. That one was taken by the newspaper when he made all-state. Self-conscious graduation portraits in living color. My parents' wedding picture—taken how many years ago—29, 30? How young they looked.

I studied it, thinking Dad hadn't changed that much. Older, thinner, more angular—but Mom must have put on at least 50 pounds. She used to be very pretty, even though the too-dark lipstick made her lips look bruised.

A new addition was an enlarged color snapshot of Frank with his wife, Marie, and their baby daughter, Carol. The first, and so far only, grandchild. None of us had yet seen her. Steady, reliable Frank, who was expected to take over Dad's store someday, had preferred to open a garage in California.

Once again the memory of our parents' reaction to his betrayal stirred mixed emotions in my gut. Anger, understanding, and more than a little guilt at my own desire to get away. With a sigh, I left the display and went to bed.

I woke to an empty house. Dad I knew would be at the store, and a note from Mom told me she was out shopping.

Scribbling "gone to see Paula" at the bottom of the Post-it Note, I filled a mug with coffee and headed for the car.

Trees, brilliant as a Van Gogh painting, overhung the streets. The air was hazy with the burn-off of a lost summer. I drove with windows open, sniffing the fragrance of smoldering leaves. Eventually I came to an almost-new development of houses with hard-to-see numbers, squatting on stingy lawns. They looked so much alike, it was hard to remember which one was Paula's. I pulled to a hesitant stop.

Behind a chain-link fence a toddler in a bright red jumpsuit stumbled after a puppy. His chubby body shook with laughter as the dog gamboled just out of reach. When the child finally tumbled into a heap, he lay still except for one slowly kicking foot. The puppy circled him, sniffing, then licked his face. I was shocked at the intensity of my yearning to pick him up, hold him tight.

When a red-haired young woman in slacks and sweater came around the corner of the house, I scrambled out of the car. Wildly waving one arm in the air, I called out "Paula."

She stopped. Stared, then rushed to open the gate and gave me a hug. "Kathy. It's so good to see you."

"Your baby. Tommy, isn't it? I can't get over how big he is."

We walked to the house, recalling our last meeting when her belly looked big enough to explode. Laughed over the baby shower where a cluster of ribbons had promised twins. Almost three years ago.

Once inside, Paula disappeared into the kitchen, insisting on refreshments as she kept up a steady chatter I could barely hear. I took in the scattered toys, the pint-sized ride-on plastic fire engine, the pile of partially folded laundry on the couch. The demands of a new life. I glanced out the window. Tommy was still on the ground, the puppy belly-flopped beside him. Both sound asleep. I grinned.

Paula started to set down a tray holding cokes and Oreo cookies on the coffee table. "Darn," she said, pushing aside two small cars to make room "I almost forgot. It's Tommy's naptime."

"Don't worry about it." I motioned toward the window. "He didn't." For the first time I noticed the dark smudges under her eyes, the thinness of her face, her arms. She looked exhausted.

"You have a real doll," I said.

"Yeah, and one who runs me ragged. But I wouldn't trade him for anything."

We sipped and nibbled, trying to think of something more to say. Best friends with so little left in common, we were practically strangers. My searching glance landed on a thin book that lay before a wedding picture of Big Tom and Paula ensconced in a golden frame. It looked familiar. "Isn't that Steinbeck's book, *The Pearl*?"

"Yep. Remember old Ellis, our English teacher? She gave it to us as a wedding present."

"You're kidding." I frowned, trying to remember the story. Something about a poor Mexican couple who found a great pearl. And threw it away after losing their baby.

Paula leaned forward and picked up the book. Opening it, she handed it to me without a word. On the flyleaf Ellis had written, "May your marriage always hear the song of the family."

Memory of the story flowed back in choppy waves. Possession of the pearl—promise of a better life—greed, envy, death—what had Steinbeck called it? Song of evil? Song of the family stood for man, woman, baby.

"Remember how Ellis insisted family was the very foundation of civilization?" I asked, handing it back. "So how is Big Tom?"

Silence swallowed the air. I stared at her, startled by the emotions struggling to take possession of her face. At last she said, "I don't know."

"What do you mean, you don't know?"

"Just what I said.. He's gone. Walked out."

"Oh, Paula." I can hardly believe it. They'd been inseparable all through high school; together as long as I'd known them. "How could he? What happened? Do you want to talk about it?"

She picked up a cookie with shaking fingers, Stared at it with unseeing eyes. "I think there's another woman."

"Only you're not sure."

"Come on, Kathy. What else could it be?"

I glanced around the small, messy room with its stifling air of domesticity, thinking, haven't you ever wanted to run away from all this? But I asked instead, "What are you going to do?"

"Get a divorce."

"But the baby?"

"I know. Don't you think I know?" Paula swallowed hard, fighting for control, and lost. "He didn't think of Tommy," she gulped between sobs. "He said he needed to get away, to have time to—what? Find himself? What are we supposed to live on in the meantime? Who's going to take care of Tommy if I have to go back to work?"

"You mean he hasn't sent you any money?"

"Yes. I mean, no, he has. Only how long is he going to keep it up? Almost all the money we had went into buying the house, and then Tom lost his job...." As Paula wept on my shoulder, I put my arm around her, not knowing what to say.

When the tears subsided, the words gushed forth—a flood of complaints and disparaging remarks about actions and events that struck me as being largely inconsequential. *Was it all the little things that broke up marriages*? I tried to remember the arguments Greg and I have had, and couldn't recall what started any of them.　.　.

After getting her to admit Tom must have found some kind of work in order to send any money at all, I managed to squeeze in a few practical, hardheaded words of my own. By the time I left, Paula had given me a grudging, "Okay, I'll wait. But only for a little while." Her promise gave me a ridiculous feeling of relief. It was almost as if my future happiness depended on her saving their marriage.

I took the long way back to town, lost in thought about what had happened to my friends. What a mess they'd made of what had begun as such a joyous occasion. *If Greg and I get married, will the same thing happen to us?*

The sun had dropped to a golden band shining above the horizon when I reached Main Street. Dad's old Chevrolet was still parked in front of his store. Pulling in beside it, I went inside. A boy I didn't recognize was pushing a broom over the floor between the narrow aisles. Counters were crammed with faucets, electric outlets, paint brushes, screwdrivers, and numerous small items separated by plastic dividers.

Dad was at a beat-up desk in the back room, totaling up the day's receipts. He gave me a welcome smile while his fingers continued to move across the keys.

I sat quietly in a straight backed chair with a missing rung, until he'd stapled the last of the tape to a handful of sales slips. Then I asked, "What makes a man leave his family?"

"You're talking about Tom, aren't you?"

When I nodded, he leaned back and looked past my shoulder as if the answer was written on the wall. At last he said, "He'll be back."

"What makes you so sure?"

"Two things. One, he loves his wife and son. Secondly, he couldn't live with himself if he didn't."

I watched him rise, shrug his shoulders into a denim jacket. The sudden realization he might be speaking about himself from his own experience, came as a shock. While I was growing up, my parents kept any major differences strictly between themselves. Even now I didn't dare ask.

***

I was helping Mom load the dinner plates into the dishwasher when I told her Paula's thinking of getting a divorce.

"I was afraid of that. Maybe Tom did a foolish thing, but with a baby—" she shook her head. "Young people are just too quick to run nowadays."

"I tried to talk her out of it and she said she'd wait awhile. Still, if push comes to shove, it shouldn't be too hard for her to start a new life."

"Bosh. I have an idea she'd find it surprisingly like the

old one."

I felt my eyebrows rise. "How can you say that? A woman has a lot more choices today. It's not as if she has to have a man just to survive. Some women even choose to have babies without having to bother with a husband."

Although her mouth pursed in disapproval, her only comment was, "She's still Paula."

"Meaning what? She's born and bred to be a housewife?"

"That's her need, Kathy."

I opened my mouth to object, then thought better of it. From what I remembered of Paula—and we'd been friends since third grade—she had never wanted to be anything else. It was me who talked of a "career", of leaving this "one-horse town" for the unknown city.

True, I had found an excitement in the theatre, arts, museums, night spots, stores and restaurants a town like Hopeville could never know. But I'd also found my job as an executive assistant was routine, my friends few, and my home a dingy two rooms and bath at an exorbitant price. The best thing to come out of the eight years, was meeting Greg. .

Above the swish of the dishwasher, the hum of the refrigerator, I could hear bursts of subdued laughter and applause from the TV in the living room. Common, everyday sounds of home. The boring routine we run from, yet long to return to after we've escaped. Once again I thought of Steinbeck's book, *The*

Pearl. A wry grin twisted my lips as I recalled the point of the story. At the end, the woman who had always walked behind the man, was by his side when he threw the pearl into the sea.

It was then I knew I would marry Greg. I laughed out loud as an invisible weight seemed to drop from my shoulders. "Mom," I said, "I'm going back."

She looked at me in disbelief. "Tonight? Kathy, it's past eight o'clock and the drive—"

"I know." I gave her a quick hug, thinking if she knew what this was all about, she'd shove me out the door. "Don't worry. I'll be fine."

I ran into the hall and up the stairs to collect my things. Thinking, if he's asleep—and no doubt he will be—I'll wake him. To tell him *Greg, my love, now is the time for singing.*

St. Anthony Messenger. November, 2002

6

THE BOTTLE

The pale green bottle bobbed beneath a thin layer of suds. With a sigh, Allison began to pick at the labels, swearing under her breath as the words "Chenin Blanc" clung to the glass. Beneath the scratching of fingernail and scouring pad, the glue reluctantly released its hold. "Government warning...", "percentage of alcohol..." floated to the surface in shredded bits of paper. When she turned the bottle upside down to drain, her hand paused in mid-air. Fine golden hairs seemed to rise on her arms, the back of her neck as she thought, *I've done this before.*

Only she hadn't. Allison stared at the bottle, willing it to explain the sensation that grabbed at her with unseen fingers. Inert, empty, it gleamed in the overhead light. There was a bluish cast to the green glass when she turned it so....

******

Sunlight filtered through the mist. A field of tiny green plants stretched row upon row, as far as her eye could see. Each plant at her feet had a tight round head and she knelt to examine one. What she thought looked like a Brussels sprout, resembled a face with the mouth and eyes closed. As if it were sleeping.

A building on the horizon had a hip roof but no windows. She rose and began to walk toward it, picking her way between the rows. With each step she felt as if her feet were lifting in the air. So weightless, she imagined she was walking on the moon. By the time she reached it her breath came in gasps, and a thin film of sweat covered her skin.

Although the structure seemed to be made of unpainted wood, not a grain, seam or knothole marred its surface. Allison reached out a curious hand. Despite the lack of any visible sign, a door opened before her. She stepped into an enclosed space the size of a walk-in closet. A low rumble sounded behind a second door, that had a knob.

She opened it onto a cavernous room, the walls lined from floor to ceiling with assorted electronic equipment. Buttons and dials, analog and digital displays, levers and monitors tinted amber, blue, and green contained multi-colored graphs. Printers piled up ream after ream of paper on the tiled floor. Allison stared, open-mouthed, wondering what she had stumbled into.

Before she could pull her thoughts together, a voice yelled out "Hey you! What are you doing here?"

Her head turned with a jerk. A fairly short, heavy-set man with a straggly gray beard, stood in the far corner. "I-I don't know."

He advanced toward her, intense blue eyes flashing in anger, and she shrank back. Thrusting out a hand, he squeezed a fold of flesh on her upper arm with stubby fingers. Surprise flooded his face, filled his voice as he asked "How did you get here?"

She held out her hands, palms up. "I don't even know where I am."

"Why it's the Garden, of course."

In silence, they looked each other over. He wore a white shirt with a faint blue stripe, open at the neck. Highly polished cowboy boots shone beneath tailored gray slacks. What remained of his brown hair was flecked with silver, yet she sensed a youthful vigor. At last he said, "I'm Gabe," and held out his hand.

Beneath her fingers his skin felt unexpectedly smooth, oddly cool. "Allison Smith." Her glance traveled around the room. "I saw the plants outside, but all these…"

"This is a huge operation. With only two assistants, it has to be fully automated."

"What do you grow here?"

"Grow? We don't grow anything."

"But all those plants…and you said 'garden.' "

His blue eyes deepened in color. A twinkle spread from their corners and his lips twitched. "You really don't know what's going on, do you." He was trying hard not to laugh. Finally Gabe said, "We recycle."

"You mean this is where all the papers, cans and bottles end up?"

This time his laughter broke into loud guffaws. When reduced to an occasional chuckle, he said, "We recycle spirits. This is the Garden of Eternal Life."

A prickly sensation swept over Allison as the words sank in. Her mind whirled and each minute hair from her head to her toes, stood at attention.

Gabe took her arm and pointed to a display of letters and figures that lined one wall. All the letters were stationary, but the digits changed at various speeds. It looked like a thousand digital clocks run amok. He picked up a pointer and placed the tip at the end of a line that read DA followed by a string of numbers. The last two digits were turning over at a rapid rate.

"Still at it," he muttered, half to himself, before he explained, "The DA stands for Darfur; the figures show how many are dying at this particular moment."

With a glazed expression, Allison's eyes followed the pointer to a matching set of letters. Here the digits were changing at a much slower rate.

"These numbers," Gabe said, " represent births. Same time, same place. Looks like we'll have to ready another field."

"I—I don't understand."

"Simple, really. Supply and demand. When there are more deaths than births, we have to plant the spirits of the dead until there is a reversal in the cycle."

It's crazy, she thought. Totally, unbelievably mad.

"Wars are bad enough," Gabe was saying, "but natural disasters like earthquakes and tsunamis that can kill hundreds of thousands, those are what screw up the operation."

His eyes pleaded for her to picture the tremendous influx of spirits piling up at the entrance, clamoring to be admitted, as he tried to describe the indescribable. "…so many to get through the intake procedure. There were fights, and then," his eyes rolled heavenward, "the computers went down." Gabe grimaced at the memory. "Believe you me, that was pure hell."

Drawn by his words, Allison imagined a mountain of Brussel sprouts bobbing and bumping into each outside the building. *Only, spirits are ethereal, without substance. Aren't they?* In desperation she grabbed at a bit of what she recalled. "There's an intake procedure?"

"Yeah. These numbers just give the amount and location. We have to make sure they match up, that none are missing, or we have more than we're supposed to get. Then there's all that other information…"

"Like race? Sex? Serial number?

His eyes flashed a reprimand, but all he said was, "We're talking spirits here, not bodies."

"Then it doesn't matter whether a person was male or female? Black, yellow, whatever?"

"That's right. For example, those coming from Darfur will be processed and placed wherever a baby has been started anywhere in the world."

"But you said other information?"

"A lot of these spirits have been around a long time. We have to clean them up, get rid of excess baggage, so to speak."

"Like wipe out the memories?"

Gabe shook his head. "Those they keep. But some of 'em—well, we're supposed to find the bad seed."

"You're sure not doing so hot with that one."

"We can't find 'em all," he admitted. "Just too many people nowadays. I told the Boss we can't keep up, I need more help. A bigger place, more and better equipment, like some of these new machines…"

He sounded so much like her husband, she could picture the Boss passing off the complaints with an impatient gesture. Probably saying, *if you'd get off your butt…* A grin tugged at the corners of her mouth. Gabe was still talking. His lips moved, but she couldn't hear—She leaned forward, straining to make out what he was saying…

and found herself looking at two pots of African violets above her on the window sill. The blooms were wilted. Allison blinked. With a quick shake of her head she glanced around the room. At fruit-shaped magnets tacked recipes, crayoned drawings, and scribbled notes on the refrigerator door. A highchair and dinette table that bore signs of a recent meal. Through the opening to the family room she could see Tim sprawled on the couch, engrossed in Monday night football. Looking down, Allison found her right hand wrapped around the neck of the bottle. Gabe slowly disappeared beneath the glass.

With a bemused sigh, she placed it on the counter and went to check on the children.

7

WHICH WAVELENGTH ARE YOU ON?

"More coffee?"

Of course he wants more coffee. She knows it is as stupid a question as his response. No words. Not even a look. Just a grunt and rattle of newspaper. Betty fills his mug, then eyes the time. 7:32. At exactly eight o'clock George will leave for the fifteen minute drive to Foley Manufacturing where he heads the accounting department. She wonders what he would do if some unforeseen obstacle made him five minutes late.

Her cup matches the dishes. Dusky rose. His mug is white with Good Morning Lover! written in red. *Who's he kidding?* "I'm going to get you a new mug," she says. "I saw a cute one in Country Fare. It had My Favorite Grandpa on it."

The newspaper seems to shrink an d curl at the edges. His grunt comes out as "Oh God…" George glances at his watch and folds the paper into a neat rectangle. He runs a hand over brown hair touched with gray, and trying to escape a high forehead.

Once on his feet he hitches the belt stretched around a corpulent middle, followed by an absent-minded check of the fly.

"See you tonight," he says, pecking the air near her cheek.

It is her turn to grunt. Elbows propped on the table, Betty sips her coffee as the sound of his 1987 shiny new Ford Mustang leaves the driveway. Her 1979 Chevy 4-door behind the garage doors is beginning to rust.

"Damn," she mutters finding another stain on the front of her robe. Grape jelly, already embedding it's purple shade into the fabric. *What difference does it make?* With a shrug, she reaches for the paper and pulls out the comics. George wouldn't notice if she came to the table in the nude.

***

Grandpa. The word knocks on the door of his mind demanding entrance, as George struggles just as hard to keep it out. My God, I'm only fifty-five, how could Debby do this to him? Damn it, she and Mike have only been married—what? Two-three years?

George Jr. arrived nine months and six days after he and Betty said "I do."

That was different.

At the light, an old man with stringy white hair and a cane limps in front of him. He has a crazy urge to run him down, toss him into oblivion. As if the act could stop time in its tracks. Lips held tight he swings the wheel in an angry turn onto El Prado.

George pulls into the driveway of a concrete block house painted a pale green, and leans on the horn. A couple appear in the doorway. The man is of average height with hair the color of sand. One hand carries an attaché case. The woman is wearing a robe splashed with large red flowers. He watches their farewell kiss with disinterest, thinking she looks as sloppy as Betty. Two of a kind. They have been friends with Alan and Jane Martin ever since they met at a Foley Christmas party years ago He and Alan, an engineer, have carpooled ever since.

"What are you looking so grim about?" Alan asks, settling into the passenger seat.

"My daughter's turning me into an old man."

"How? What did she do, for God's sake?"

"She got pregnant" A smile trembles at the edge of George's mouth. "I just remembered what my father said when we told him about George, Jr. 'I don't. mind being a grandfather half as much as being married to a grandmother."

"I hear you."

The hell you do, George thinks, suspecting the only child Alan has is a fag.

"Did you read about the big layoff Handiwell's just had?" Alan frowns. "What's happened to our economy anyway? It's beginning to sound like it's the Depression our parents went through." Alan looks down at his hands as he asks, "How's Foley doing? I heard we're in the market for a takeover. Are we?"

"Not that I know of." *Maybe you ought to ask my assistant. To think I took him under my wing...*"Of course sales are down, that happens. But it's no reason to believe every rumor you hear."

"I think we better put our wives back to work."

"You may be right. If we can ever pry them loose from those stupid soaps."

Alan breaks the silence with "What do you think of Johnson's new secretary? Pretty hot, right?"

"She reminds me of Pam. *" It was happening a lot lately, the memory of what she did with her hands, her mouth—George* licks his lips, glares at the light that forces him to a stop. *Why can't Betty want it when I'm ready instead of turning her back? Or acting like she'd doing me a favor. Why can't she...*

"...as long as no one gets hurt, I always say. Right?"

George hears enough to know Alan is referring to Judy, a pert little redhead he's been involved with the past six months. He glances at his friend, torn once more between curiosity and envy. "You really think it's worth the risk?"

"The way she makes me feel? Hell, yes." They pull into Foley's parking lot. "To Jane, I'm no more than a meal ticket. To Judy, "his smile reflects a secret memory, "I'm a man."

***

'...body arched against his long, passionate kisses that demanded total surrender. Trembling with a desire pushed beyond control, she cried out "Take me. Oh my darling, take me now." With a muffled groan he buried his face between her breasts as she willingly parted her...'

The phone rings. Betty closes the paperback with a muffled "Damn." Beneath its title *Passion's Fruit* a lusty young couple embraced in vibrant color. If only George would—dropping the book on the couch she picks up the receiver.

"Am I speaking with Mrs. George Bailey?"

"Yes," she admits warily, trying to place the caller.

"I have great news for you, Mrs. Bailey. You have just won..."

Lord, not another salesman. Betty starts to hang up. Pauses. The voice on the other end of the line is male. Warm and seductive. Sexy. She lets him continue his spiel, not hearing the words but the deep, honeyed tone that paints a mental picture. *Dark and muscular with bold, black eyes. Like the one on the book cover. And she—young and slim, her full breasts pressing against a tight low-cut bodice as his strong hands...*

She realizes he has stopped talking. Did he ask her a question? "What? I'm sorry but would you repeat that? We seem to have a poor connection."

"I asked, Mrs. Bailey, if we could make an appointment that I might show you our product. I'm sure once you see—"

Resisting the urge to say "It depends on what you intend to show", Betty breaks in with "I'm sorry, but I'm really not interested."

Good Lord, what's wrong with me? she wonders, quickly hanging up. I can't believe I was actually imagining making love with a complete stranger. .

Shaken, she collects a dustcloth and mop from the utility room. Perhaps if she concentrates on housework she can erase the temptation.

***

The new secretary has her eyes on the computer screen. George's gaze lingers over shiny blonde hair that falls to her shoulders, the soft curve of her cheek, a slight tilt to a nose above lips where a faint pout holds a tantalizing invitation. I can always take her to lunch, he thinks. A nice gesture of welcome. Strictly business, of course. He straightens his tie. Steps forward and says, "Good morning, Shelley."

She turns. Eyes the color of cornflowers make him catch his breath. How fresh and young she looks, he thinks. Untouched. Almost virginal. *Don't be an ass.*

"Good morning, Mr. Bailey." Her smile shows even white teeth. "Can I help you?"

Baby, can you ever. He swears she is not wearing a bra. *Shadows beneath the shirt shrink and tighten into quivering buds as his hands stroke, caress*—George clears his throat. "Yes. I'm looking for Johnson's monthly report. Have you finished the run yet?"

A perplexed look crosses her face. "Why yes, sir. I gave it to Mr. Stone yesterday morning."

All thought of their having lunch together flees before her words. Russ. Unease twists his gut. *Why hasn't he given it to me? It should have been on my desk yesterday. That little fart is after my job...*

"Thank you, Shelley," he mutters, and strides toward his office. It is one of the few that still has walls and a window in a building where open space is broken up by partitions. Closing the door behind him, he buzzes Russ on the intercom.

The man who enters is tall, with the curly dark brown hair women like to play with. Good build. Big on fitness, George thinks, irritated that he can't remember the last time he worked out in the company weight room. Resenting most of all that Russ is more than twenty years younger than he.

"Here are all the monthly reports," Russ says, before he can open his mouth.

George glares at the neat pile of printouts placed on his desk. "Mmmmph," he grunts. "I heard you picked up Purchasing's yesterday morning. Why didn't I see this then?"

"I just presumed you'd want all the information together and summarized. As usual."

George turns his glare on the papers before him. "Good job. Thanks," he finally admits, begrudging each word.

"Want me to go over the figures with you?"

Heat is rising under the collar of his shirt. *Think I'm too old to handle it?* "I'll take it from here," he says and reaches for the top sheet. George misses the smirk on Russ's face when he turns to leave.

The figures are even worse than he'd imagined. A big drop in sales for the third month in a row. Too high an inventory—he'd warned Johnson to cut back on the buying. Why hadn't he done it? And the payroll—a spasm ripples through his gut as he thinks of the suggestions he'll have to make to his boss. Based on this report.

Could Russ have made a mistake? If he did it would reflect as much, maybe more, on himself for not having caught it. George begins to study the figures in earnest.

Russ has done a damn good job. Too good, if errors were what he's been hoping for. Wearily, he rises and walks to the window. Past a sea of cars he can spot a sliver of green-brown grass containing a single straggly tree. Beyond it the sky is filmed in pewter gray without color or light. It matches his mood.

Why wouldn't he be worried?. His department may be one of the most efficient, but at fifty-five he is one of the oldest employees left in the whole damn plant. George thinks of when he was hired twenty-eight years ago and his mind climbs onto a roller-coaster of memories. Eager, ambitious, smart. Anxious to "help" the "old man". The one he later displaced.

What a high that was. His grin widens as he recalls his promotion, the way Betty looked at him. As if he were some kind of God. Now—his forehead creases in a scowl. Where is the Betty who was pretty and feminine and loving? Who was lively, fun to be with? Dragging around all day in a ratty robe, that's where. Without makeup Or perfume. She used to look so nice, give me a big kiss when I got home from work...

The image of long blonde hair, unbound breasts, flashes across his mind. His face softens. George looks at his watch. .12:08. Maybe he can still catch her. He slips on his jacket. Straightens his tie and walks out the door. Shelley's desk is empty. She has already left.

***

The trouble with housework, Betty thinks, flipping a cloth over an end table, is it requires so little mental effort. Always the same routine; do the dishes, dust, mop, vacuum, shop, make supper, set the table. Watch your man fall asleep in front of TV night after night. Week after week. Month after month. It was different when the kids were growing up. Then things were so hectic she'd wonder if she'd get anything done. A long time ago...

Her glance travels over the room. The faint sheen of waxed tables, a spray of plastic flowers before a mirror, a painted sunset above the couch. All so spotless not one dust mote dances in the air. So quiet the silence hangs like a pall. "Maybe," Betty says, "I need to find me a job."

It isn't the first time this idea has occurred to her. Just reading about the sheer number of working women is enough to make her feel out of step. Only what can she do? It's been years since she'd drawn a paycheck. Ever since George began making good money and she let him talk her into staying home and be a real wife and mother.

Okay so she didn't exactly object to the idea then. But now she's past fifty and when she watches TV, the women seem to be doctors, lawyers, or detectives. Married fresh out of high school, she'd been a salesclerk in a department store.

"What kind of a job?" Jane had asked her that when she first admitted looking at the classifieds a few months ago. "I don't know," she'd said then. The same answer she'd say today.

"Dunkin' Donuts is looking for help," Jane had told her, biting into one.

"And " she'd replied, "there's probably a thousand people applying for it,"

The subject finally closed when Jane had asked "Does George know about this?"

George. He'd been so proud, so pleased when she'd agreed to quit work. "Bringing in the money is my job," he'd said. "Yours is to keep me happy." .

They'd been so young then. Betty reaches for the mop. Still so much in love For a brief moment memories have them laughing as they ran up a hill. He catching her, falling together in sweet-smelling grass. Kissing. The warmth if the sun, the heat of their bodies… For her it was the only time the earth moved. Just like the stories promised .

Her mouth twists in a sour grimace. She changes the bed. Shaking out the perfunctory kiss George gives her before rolling over, along with the sheets. There must be something she can do to stir him up once again.

***

Foley's is fast approaching a financial crisis. Why hasn't Clem Davison called him in to discuss the situation? As the day wears on George can feel his vague unease spread into tentacles of fear. He tries fighting back with fantasies of Shelley, but she keeps slipping out of his grasp, leaving him to once again face a nameless dread.

At least it's Friday. Thank God it's Friday. Maybe Shelley will have a drink with—the page on his phone interrupts. He lifts the receiver.

"Glad I caught you," Davison says. "If you're not too busy, I'd like to see you in my office."

Finally, George thinks, rising to his feet.

Davison's office has a bank of windows. Hands clasped behind his back he is looking out at the neatly landscaped lawn. At last he turns around, a tall, thin man with a brush of black hair already sprinkled with salt. George sees no welcome smile in his flat gray eyes

"Have a seat." Davison remains standing. He shuffles a few papers on the desk. Its polished surface holds a gold pen and pencil set on a solid marble base, and a phone.

George shifts uneasily in his chair.

"You above all, George, know the situation Foley Manufacturing is facing."

"The company's faced worse before and made it through," George hastens to say. *How much of company history does Davison really know? He's only been here five-six years. A "wunderkind" who made general manager before he was 40. By the time he gets to be my age he'll be CEO.* Swallowing a bitter taste he adds, "In the past we handled it by…"

Davison's hand makes an impatient gesture. "In the past there was half the number of employees and one third the production with little automation. This is a brand new ballgame."

.   "Some things don't change. I think if we…"

"Cut back the fat. Become lean and mean."

George feels his stomach lurch. "Yes. That's what I meant, but..."

Davison sits down. Looks at his desk. "Twenty-eight years," he says softly. "A long time to stick with one company nowadays." He raises his eyes, focuses on George. Pinning him to the chair. "And don't think we aren't grateful for both your loyalty and exemplary work. Now we think it's time for you to take it easy and enjoy life."

His stomach seems to have no bottom. George stares at him, unable to speak.

"Foley's has put together an excellent retirement package," Davison goes on.

"I'm only fifty-five years old, for Christ's sake."

"Excellent," Davison repeats, ignoring the outburst. "For someone at your level we offer..."

The list of benefits fade in and out of George's mind. He feels sick. Numb. Unable to think, to retaliate. Davison has come around the desk. Is pressing the packet into his hands.

"I believe you'll find this very generous," he says. "Read it over the weekend. Then if you have any questions..."

"You mean when I come in on Monday—"

"If you need to talk with Personnel. Or me, of course." He places a hand on George's shoulder. "By now everyone should have left the building. I imagine you'd rather be alone to clean out your things?" He gives the shoulder a squeeze. "You can't know how much I regret—"

George looks at him, then at the hand. Removing it with his own, he turns and leaves the office without another word.

***

George pulls to a stop at the edge of the parking lot for one last look. At his office hidden in an addition to the old brick building that has worn the black letters Foley Manufacturing Company on its roof since 1934. The memorabilia of his sojourn are stuffed into a single carton in the back seat. A few books, pictures of Betty and the kids, when they really were kids, and one of he and Hayes, the former GM together with old Foley himself. A framed award—small waves of grief, pain, loss begin to whisper against the shore of his mind. Blinking rapidly, he steps on the gas. He needs a drink.

The lounge is dark, crowded, familiar. George takes an empty stool nearest the door. He doesn't notice a sudden drop in the noise level.

"The usual, Mr. Bailey?"

"Yeah, Bud. Wait. Make it a double."

His eyesight is growing accustomed to the gloom. A reflection in the mirror behind the bar makes him freeze. Russ is crowded into a booth with other coworkers. Celebrating his, Russ's promotion. Looking at him, George, the loser. Without averting his eyes, he reaches for his drink Holds it up in a silent toast to the victor, and tosses it down. To burn its way through the knot of bitter gall stuck in his throat. Only then does he turn and walk out the door.

George pulls into traffic with an angry swerve of the wheel. The little fart. Thanks to him I can't even get drunk. Aware, even as he thinks it, that there are other bars. But what's the point? So he drinks himself into a stupor, it still won't change the facts. He's become a useless old man.

Alan. He'd forgotten all about him. Was he in the bar? If he knew what happened his friend would probably want to avoid him. That it might be catching. Early retirement, my foot. He was fired. Tossed out to make room for the young Turks. .

Oh God, how can he tell Betty? He can hear her now— she'll *say Fifty-five isn't old, you'll be able to get another job, A better one.*

His lip curls and he mutters, "Get with it, woman." Can't you understand? Your ever-loving husband is beat up, dried out. Finished.

George unexpectedly finds himself thinking of her body, the way it has grown plumper over the years. Softer, more comfortable. Like a pillow. He turns into their driveway, suddenly anxious to lay his head on her breast. To feel her arms around him, holding him. Protecting him. Rocking him like she had their babies. Like his mother used to do with him.   .

The door opens as he makes the top step, and he jerks to a stop. Stunned. Staring. *Betty?*

The apparition before him has light red hair that curls around a face—a palette for blue eye shadow, pink cheeks, and bright red lips. Long black lashes surround gray-green eyes. Her perfume snakes around his head, assaults his nose. Beneath a sheer black gown he never saw before, the woman is naked.

"Welcome home, lover," she says in a throaty voice ala Lauren Bacall. Her outstretched hand holds a martini.

What the hell? George hesitates, tempted to bolt. Unsure whether to laugh or cry.

"Come." She beckons with the cocktail. "I have something for you."

There's a faint stirring in his groin. *Okay, So he was looking for mama and gets Blaze Starr.* Intrigued in spite of himself, George reaches for his drink and follows her inside.

8

THE CARD GAME

Angie Davis stares at the 13 cards she holds in her left hand. The fingers on her other hand curl strands of hair behind her right ear as she thinks Christ, it's been too long since—why did I set up this bridge game anyway? Her glance strays around the table where each place holds the occupants favorite drink. Scotch and soda for Dave. Perrier water with a lime for Lena. A Cuba Libre for Chuck. White wine for herself. Two small dishes of mixed nuts balance precariously in opposite corners.

They used to play a lot--she, Dave and Chuck, when they were neighbors. Before the guys moved out of the complex. Before Dave got married. Again. With a sigh, she concentrates on her hand. Let's see, how many points for an opening bid? Two aces—that's eight--a queen and jack of hearts—three more--only one diamond...

"Well? We don't have all night..."

She turns to Dave, seated on her left. Frowns as she notes the loose belly and veined, bulbous nose of a heavy drinker. *Why should I notice that now when it never bothered me before?* "Don't bug me. I'm counting."

He grimaces, reaches for his glass.

"One heart," Angie says, then wonders why she opened her mouth. She tries to catch her partner's eye, to mentally beg her to pass, but Lena does not look up.

"Two diamonds," Dave says.

"Two hearts." The deep drag Lena takes on her cigarette ends in a hacking cough.

Angie stifles a groan. She turns hopeful eyes on Chuck who seems to be somewhere out in left field. *I've caught the way he looks at me...is he still trying to think up ways to get me into bed when the evening ends? He's bound to have gotten the message by now...* "Chuck? It's your turn."

He starts. "Sorry." Glances at his cards. "I pass."

Crossing mental fingers that Lena will get her signal, Angie does the same.

Dave quirks an eyebrow in her direction. Glares at Chuck. "Three spades."

Lena's response of "Four hearts" has the impact of a rifle shot. Angie's eyes dart arrows at her partner but Lena's are fastened on those of her husband. Turning from her to Dave, Angie wonders, *What's with these two?. Does she know about him and me? But that's been over for...* She bites her lip to keep from begging Dave to get her off the hook. She used to count on that, his competitiveness, his skill with cards that could turn even her stupid bids into a win. When he was her partner.

But now a smirk sneaks across his face. "Double."

Lena lays down her cards in four vertical rows, facing Angie. Her words, "It's all yours, partner" are broken up in a fit of coughing.

One look at the display and Angie wants to scream, *why in God's name didn't you pass to begin with?*

Unperturbed, Lena leans back in her chair. The clothes that hang on her body tremble as if moved by an unseen wind. Cigarette smoke rises around a face Angie suddenly realizes is pale and drawn. So gaunt the cheekbones stick out like a pair of miniature shoulder blades.

"Damn it Lena, when are you gonna quit smoking?" Dave's voice is rough, but his brown eyes are filled with concern. "She keeps us both awake half the night," he complains to the table at large, as he leads with a diamond.

"Maybe I'll stop smoking when you give up drinking," Lena says. She stands, looks at Angie. "If it's okay with you, I'll step outside while you play the hand."

Angie gives an indifferent nod, as anger mixed with despair glues her eyes to the cards.

Dave reaches for his drink and drains it. "Hey, you're dummy," he tells his wife, holding up the empty glass. "How about a refill before you go?"

Lena's answer is a dirty look. She walks to the front door, slams it behind her.

Chuck grins. "Looks like you'll have to wait. Or get it yourself."

"That cough does sound pretty bad," Angie says, conceding her single diamond to Dave's queen. "What does the doctor say?"

"I can't get her to go."

"You're kidding. Why not?"

Dave shrugs. "She doesn't think much of doctors ever since one of her kids almost died years ago. Misdiagnosis. What am I supposed to do? Hog-tie and drag her there?"

"Maybe if I talk with her...?"

"Would you do that?"

"Why not? I like your wife. Don't know if it'll do any good, but I'm willing to try."

"Bless you." Dave grabs for her free hand and gives it a sloppy kiss.

"Yuck," Angie says, wiping the back of her hand on her skirt.

"You didn't use to act like that..." Memories warm their

smiles. Angie lifts her glass in a small salute, then turns back to the game.

***

Angie finds Lena leaning against the balcony railing . "Down two, doubled" she tells her, surprised it wasn't more. She rests a hand on the rusting wrought iron. "I figure it was time for a break."

A moon half-obscured by clouds drifts overhead. The scent of jasmine rises from below. "Smell that?" Lena asks, taking a deep breath. "It takes me back to the days when I first met Dave. We were college sweethearts. Did you know that?"

"So he told me." She remembers how excited he sounded. How it made her wonder if we all carry a fantasy of a past love in our hearts, over the years we are wrapped in the reality of marriage to another. With Dave, the dream must have lasted through two ex-wives.

Lena suddenly curls into a half bow and grips the rail as a relentless cough spasms her body. When the spell subsides, she gives a mirthless laugh. Says, "It's taken over 20 years for us to get back together and finally tie the knot. Only by then he's a drunk, and I'm dying."

Oh no. Angie's eyelids squeeze shut, then fly open, but Lena's face is in shadow and she can't make out her expression. "How can you be so sure? Dave says you won't go to a doctor."

"I couldn't tell him I already did. Not yet. Not when the doc said what I already knew. The Big C. Same type that killed my father."

"But there must be something...new drugs, an operation..."

"I was told where it's located it's inoperable. And as for chemo, or radiation..." Lena shrugs. Takes a drag on her cigarette. "They give me six months. Maybe a year with treatment. I'm not sure if buying a bit more time will be worth the agony."

"Maybe if you'd quit smoking...?"

"You sound just like my husband. But it's too late, so what's the point?"

"Oh, Lena. I'm so sorry."

They fall silent. At last Lena says, "Do you know where I can find some grass?"

"What?"

"You know, weed. Whatever they call it now. Marijuana. I haven't had any since college, but I read somewhere it's got some medical benefit--eases pain or something. Only my doctor said he can't prescribe it. It's still against the law around here, and I thought maybe..."

Angie frowns. *Why ask me? Did Dave tell her about the time my son grew pot in the attic and someone called the cops?* She recalls the big to-do over a recent drug bust, and is tempted to suggest Lena try the police. Her mouth twists in a wry smile at the thought, but she asks, "Know any high school kids?"

"Nope. There is a school near us, and don't think I haven't thought of going up to one of 'em and asking. With my luck I'd probably get the one kid who would turn me in to the principal." Her rueful laugh sounds like a sharp bark.

Again they fall silent. Remembering her own college years, Angie is surprised she's become so out of touch. Wonders if she should call Gary, that maybe her son can give her a name...

"Will you take back Dave when I'm gone?"

Angie is so startled, it takes a moment for her mind to focus on the sudden change of topic. *Of course she knows, Dave and his big mouth...Bigger ego. Didn't he realize the fun times they shared was all it ever was? Fun and games. Besides, once a door is shut...*Angie shakes her head before she remembers Lena won't be able to see her in the dark. "No." she says.

"I didn't suppose you would." Lena sighs, "Poor Dave" and flips the cigarette stub over the railing.

Seeing the glowing end arc through the air makes Angie think of a tiny falling star. Without another word she turns and follows Lena through the door to her apartment. Back to the game.

9

CIRCUMSTANTIAL EVIDENCE

The lounge is dimly lit, heavy with dark wood. When he and Anne first met in the lobby she'd acted stiff, nervous. They'd circled each other like strangers, as if the past had never existed. Now looking into eyes so blue they border on purple, Peter can't block the memory of what he's lost.

She's developed edges, he thinks, studying the planes of her face, the way her hair is now a short black cap, hugging her head. It's hard to ignore the phantom sensation of long tresses that once brushed his chest.

Anne's red-tipped fingers play with her drink as she says, "Boris Epstein will see you at 8:45 tomorrow morning, sharp. He has to catch a plane for California so don't be late."

"Where's his office?"

"82nd floor, Sears Tower. About five blocks from here. You must have seen it. It's still the tallest building downtown."

"82 floors? And I think Tampa's erecting skyscrapers. I'm beginning to feel like a hick in the big city."

Anne chuckles, a low sexy sound that echoes in his groin. He grins, relieved to see she's relaxing. "I knew I could count on you," he says. "As usual, you saved my life."

"And you exaggerate. As usual."

"Not this time. You've saved my job, and that's practically the same thing."

"Aren't you being a bit premature?"

He frowns. "You told me Epstein was good for the money."

"I'm thinking of Sanderson."

Arthur Sanderson. His frown deepens. The reason he, Peter Wetherby, is now CEO of the company and Anne lives in Chicago. "The only heirs the Old Man's got is a nephew interested in living off the profits without doing any of the work. Sanderson should be happy to sell the business to me instead of strangers."

"Unless they come up with a better offer."

He can feel the sweat bead up in his armpits. "Come on, Anne. We're talking small company here."

"Who's just developed a product that promises big bucks."

"That no one else but you knows about." He stares at her. "Or do they?"

Her chin lifts along with her eyebrows. "Do you think Epstein would give you the time of day, much less money if I didn't tell him?"

He looks down at his drink and mumbles, "I'm sorry. You're right." He picks up the glass, swallows. Sets it back on the table. "Maybe I'm getting paranoid, but so much is hanging..."

"I know. But you should know better..."

The words sting, lashing the image of her to life. When she'd been the best assistant he'd ever had. And as his lover, gave him two years of happiness he ended in duplicity, shame and regret. His eyes close as memory bites into his skin.

"How's Elizabeth?"

He blinks "As well as can be expected." Anxiety and guilt take over his gut. He hadn't wanted to leave her alone, but he was running out of time...Why had Ruth been delayed? Why hadn't she called if she knew she'd be late?

"She can still manage to get around okay?"

Peter looks down at the table. The top is scarred. "This past year she's become almost completely crippled." When she was diagnosed she was 26 years old, still young enough to feel immortal. That was ten years ago. His throat closes over the words, "She no longer wants to live."

"Oh dear God, how terrible. What happened?"

"She gave up when she found she couldn't get out of bed." Anne's hand closes over his and he hears Elizabeth whisper, "Promise me you will not let me live on as a vegetable." He clings to Anne's fingers. "I never expected to be in love with two women at the same time."

"Don't. Please."

"I can't help it. I love you Anne, have never stopped loving you. I should never have let you go."

"Stop it. We didn't have a choice."

But I did, he thinks, as once again he hears Sanderson tell him to either get his pen out of company ink, or forget about any promotion. He glances at Anne who is studying her drink. Did she know at the time he was being groomed for the CEO spot?

She must have known. Or at least faced the fact he was a married man who would not—could not—leave his wife. And she deserves a husband and family of her own.

"When are you and Brian going to quit playing house and make it official?"

Her eyes widen. "How did you know about him?"

"I've got my ways."

Anne turns her head, then back to look him in the eye. "In that case maybe you already know I told him to leave three months ago?"

"Really? I didn't know you two had split." Peter smothers a grin, glances around the room. Dusk has fallen and the lounge is beginning to fill up for the happy hour. He turns to Anne.. "But since you don't have to rush home to him, how about joining me for dinner?"

He orders steak, "so rare it still bleeds". She, shrimp. While they eat Anne tells him about the influential people she meets as an investment broker, her apartment, the friends she's made. He listens, and hears his desire for her rise with the all-too-real images of past love making.

Later, dancing at a nightclub, the talk changes to mutual murmurs, remembrances of times they'd shared. Holding her soft body in his arms, breasts pressed against his chest, acts like a flaming match flung into a sun-dried field. Beyond control.

It's close to midnight when they return to the hotel. Except for a bored night clerk and an elderly man dozing over a paper, the lobby is empty. Peter looks down at Anne who, face flushed, eyes shining, smiles up at him. An arm around her waist, he guides her across the marble floor to the elevators.

The hotel is old, his room showing its age like a well-preserved but hopelessly out-of-date matron. Anne takes in the carved mahogany chairs and pedestal table, the queen size bed beneath innocuous prints. Without a word she turns and holds out her arms.

He walks into them, pulling her close. Buries his nose in the flower garden of her scent. Reaches for her waist, her back, her hair, tilting her head back to kiss her neck as she whispers, "It's been so long, so very long," against his cheek.

Way too long, he thinks, afraid he'll be unable to maintain control. This night may be all they can have, but it belongs to them. He wants it to last.

***

"Peter. Peter, wake up."

Something is shaking him, a voice coming from a distance. At a poke in the ribs he opens one eye to peer into Anne's face above him.

"It's ten after seven," she says, "and you have that meeting with Epstein in less than an hour. Remember?"

He shakes his head to clear it. Opens both eyes to see her sitting cross-legged on the bed. He reaches for her. "I'd rather remember last night."

She pulls back. "You know there's no time." Her deep blue eyes are luminous. "But we had a night I won't forget..." she says so softly he barely hears the words.

His eyes drink in the glow of her nakedness. Radiant, like a bride, he thinks and the yearning to have her with him, to make her his own becomes almost unbearable. "If this deal goes through will you come back to work with me?"

A shadow passes over her face. In the sudden chill he blurts, "Oh God, Anne, I'm sorry. I don't know what I was thinking. It's just that... oh, hell I want you with me. I love you. And I don't want to lose you too."

The import of his last words sink in and they stare at each other in shock. It's one thing to know Elizabeth is dying but to admit it aloud...He sits up, swings his legs over the side of the bed. Drops his head in his hands, as the fact that truth does not always bring acceptance hits him. Nor does it eliminate the sour taste of betrayal. *My God, did he just ask for his wife's replacement before she's even in the ground?*

Anne, in half-slip and bra, is putting on her makeup and he's pulling on his trousers when there's a knock on the door. He turns to her, raises an eyebrow, momentarily wondering if it's Brian. But that's stupid—At a louder, more impatient knock, he opens the door part way. The two men standing in the hall are wearing the uniform of Chicago police.

"You Peter Wetherby?" the black cop asks.

"Yes, but..."

The officer glances at a paper in his hand. "Home address 15811 Woodlane Drive, Tampa, Florida?"

"Yes. Yes, for God's sake, what is it?"

"Wife named Elizabeth?"

He nods, sudden fear overtaking annoyance at the uniform taking so long to get to the point. For the first time he notices the second cop has wedged a foot in the door. *So he can't slam it shut in their faces? Maybe skip down the fire escape?*

That one looks to be the younger of the two. He has red hair and the build of a football linebacker. Before Peter can stop them, both men shoulder their way into the room.

"Hey," he protests, seeing Anne trying to cover herself out of the corner of his eye. "What the hell is going on?"

"Your wife was found dead, Mr. Weatherby," the second cop says, eyeing Anne with obvious interest. "Tampa police requested we bring you in on suspicion of murder."

He stares dumbly at the men, unable to comprehend what's been said. The room is tilting at a crazy angle. Anne gives a strangled cry that sounds very far away. Peter finally blurts out, "Murder my wife? You must be out of your mind. What happened? She's been ill for years, but she was alive when I left..."

"When was that?"

"Yesterday." His eyes squint as he tries to picture the time. He'd been in a hurry, running late, but the last—"I don't remember when exactly but the plane was scheduled to leave at 3:10 and the home aide..."

"Found her when she came in just before 5:30 p.m." the red-headed officer answered for him.

"5:30? Ruth was supposed to be there before I left and didn't show. I tried to reach her, couldn't get her, thought she was on her way, she'd be there after...Why was she so late?"

"You'll have to ask her. According to the report your wife supposedly died of a drug overdose sometime between three and five yesterday afternoon." The red-headed cop's eyes were a flat, emotionless gray. "According to TPD there was an empty pill bottle on the bed with one fingerprint on it. Smudged but identifiable as yours."

Of course he'd given Elizabeth her medicine before he left for the airport, he can remember that. But how many pills did he hand her? His stomach turns over as the time of death sinks in. *My God, did he kill her? No...no way. Even though she'd want him to he couldn't..*

Did he take the time to put the bottle away? Or was he in such a hurry he left it on the bedside table?

A sudden picture of Elizabeth struggling to open the bottle, forcing the pills down her throat—and then what? Wiping it with the sheet because he had touched it? Wiping off her own prints in the process. Once again he hears her whisper, "I can't bear to be a burden" and feels a weeping begin deep inside.

"You men are insane," Anne suddenly shouts. "He couldn't kill his wife. He loves her...".

He raises his head and their glances lock. The color slowly drains from her face as she realizes what he sees. What the two policemen see. What a jury would see. A married man with a beautiful mistress, and a bedridden wife who may still live for years. As a vegetable.

Peter feels as if he's been hit in the solar plexus with a battering ram. It is hard to breath. Shoulders sagging, he turns to the police. "Let me get my coat."

What else is there to say?

10

TWO FOR THE MONEY

Ten o'clock in the morning and already the day was hot
and muggy. Detective Dave Johnson wiped his brow, stuck the
handkerchief in a back pocket, and glanced once again at the
missing person report that had come in during the night. '21:36
hrs," he read, 'Amy Black…unable to reach sister, Angela Black
Walters…DOB 6/18/74…husband: John Walters…tried calling
her past three days, no answer…'

Dave cruised along Pine Street, eyes scanning for number
2111. *If she was missing why hadn't her old man made a report?*

He drove past one story houses of concrete block set on
no-longer-green lawns. From the size of the meager shade trees
planted along the sidewalk, the development couldn't be much
more than five years old. Except for an occasional bicycle, a
scatter of toys, there was no sign of life. He suddenly slowed. A
car was parked in the 2111 carport. Pulling to a stop, he reached
for his phone.

When the DMV check showed the Geo Prism was registered to one Angela Black Walters, Dave sighed with relief. False alarm he thought, reaching for the jacket slung over the back of the passenger seat. He stepped from the car, and studied the house as he shrugged it on. A few straggly bushes lined the front on each side of a small concrete stoop. What had once been flowers fenced in the bushes with dried twigs, lending a strip of dusty green and brown color to dirty white walls.

The car's here, she must be home, but there was no answer to his knock at either the front or back door. Hearing no sound from within, he walked around the house. Blinds closed off each window, so tightly shut he could not get a glimpse of what was inside.

But if she was at work, wouldn't she take the car? Frowning, he walked across the yard to the house on the right.

The old man who lived there wore thick glasses and a hearing aid. He hadn't seen Mrs. Walters "…in maybe two weeks, hadn't heard a thing." But then he admitted he'd rather look at TV than his neighbors any day of the week. At the house on the left, no one was home. The young woman who lived across the street answered the door with a baby at her shoulder. She patted it's back as she said, "We don't see either of them much. They seem like nice people but they keep pretty much to themselves." The baby burped. Dave considered it a period to the conversation, thanked her and left.

Okay, he thought, driving away. There were no reports from her boss, friends, her hubby—only her sister, who lived in another state. Her car's there, but maybe she carpools... A little visit with Mr. Walters ought to wrap it up A few blocks later he pulled into a semi-circular drive before one of two mortuaries in town. Considering the population numbered maybe 5000 if you included the dogs, one could have been enough. But what really got to him was the number of churches. Ten, at last count. He figured practically every major Christian sect must be covered.

The large brick structure had a white-columned verandah, neatly trimmed plantings, and a wide double-door of oak. "Gibson Funeral Home" was inscribed on the tasteful bronze plaque pinned to the wall. The man who answered the bell had liquid brown eyes and a thick mustache soft as a baby's breath.

"Detective Johnson," Dave said, flashing his badge. "I'm looking for a John Walters."

"Speaking. Is there a problem, detective?"

"Last night your wife was reported missing."

"Missing? Hell, she's not missing—she left me."

"Oh? When was that?"

"Five days ago."

"According to her sister, she left several messages when she called and couldn't reach her. Why didn't you tell her what happened and save us all some trouble?"

"Why should I talk to that bitch? Forget it. She never liked me, thought I wasn't good enough for her precious sister. So who was the one who walked out, tell me that."

Dave gave him a long look. *So why are you sweating?* Finally he said, "Thanks for your time." He turned to leave, paused, looked back at Walters. "Mr. Gibson. I'd like to speak with him. Is he around?"

Walters stiffened. "Mr. Gibson's away on vacation. For another week." The door closed with a slam.

And Mrs. Walters has taken off for greener pastures, Dave thought, returning to his car. Not that he could blame her. Still, there was something about Walters...Calling the station he contacted Records. "Liz, Dave. I need you to check for any DV calls on 2111 Pine St., Walters, John and Angela. Make it for last two-three years. I'll be 10-58."

He was munching on a hamburger when Liz returned his call. "One complaint, little over six months ago," she said. "Neighbor called it in. Officer Melton responded. Reported one large bruise visible on Angela's upper right arm, but victim refused any medical examination and would not press charges. That's it."

So hubby roughed her up, what-- maybe one time? Big deal. Only for some unexplainable reason Dave found he couldn't let it go.

***

"It's a puzzle," Dave said to Lieutenant Apgar that afternoon. "Walters claims she left him but her car's there. No one has seen or heard from her for almost a week. Including her co-workers. Even her boss said it wasn't like her, but when one of them called, Walters said Angela's sister was very sick and she had to leave in a hurry."

"The same sister that reported her missing?"

"Yeah, it's the only one she's got. I've also checked with the local docs, the nearest hospital, a women's shelter—and that's ten miles away. Nothing."

"A friend could have come and got her," Apgar suggested. "Or a lover. It almost sounds as if she wanted to disappear."

"Yeah, I thought of that too." Suddenly a feeling that was nagging him all day began to solidify into a definite hunch as yesterday's scene scrolled across his mind.

He was home and Barbara was loading the dishwasher . In stocking feet, and the dress she'd worn to her great-aunt's funeral. Telling him about the flowers, the service, who was there. Talking into the machine. Not that it mattered, he hadn't been listening anyway.

Now he frowned, trying to remember the exact part about Tim and the weight of the casket. When he couldn't place who Tim was, his wife had said, *My cousin, second, third, I lost*

count. But Emma was his great-grandmother. You remember
Tim, he's on the football team, a big kid, must be over six feet, a
couple hundred pounds. What struck me so funny was there must
have been five other guys lifting the coffin and Emma couldn't
have weighed more than 100 pounds when she died."

Dave grinned. He leaned forward, hands on the desk and
told Apgar what his wife's words were spelling out in his mind.
"I think," he finished," it's time to have another talk with
Walters."

Night was beginning to creep across the sky when the
front-end loader lifted Emma's coffin out of the ground. Four
spectators crowded around as the lid was raised. Dave, Apgar and
representatives from the ME and state attorney's offices peered at
skin stretched tight across the face of an old lady who'd died of
cancer. At flesh so transparent the bones showed through. Clad in
a print silk dress the body seemed to be lying on a sheet.
Working in tandem the four men lifted it up by the corners.

Angela Black Walters lay beneath Emma, her night shirt
caked in blood. Right where John Walters had said she would be
.when he finally admitted shooting her to death. Then storing her
body in the mortuary's cooler until a closed casket funeral came
along.

"That's one way to keep from paying for a burial,"
Lieutenant Apgar quipped. Dave was the only one of the four
who didn't laugh.

Futures MYSTERY Anthology Magazine, March-April, 2007

11

SMALL TOWN BLUES

A murmur of voices. Movement. I looked up from the handful of deposit slips bound by a tape with a neat row of figures. Co-workers were crowding around the First State Bank's large front window. There was Joe, dark and wiry, a holstered gun firmly strapped to his hip. Mr. Hawkins, VP of Loans, his belly sagging over his belt. Bud, one of three tellers, was practically climbing the back of scrawny, grey-haired Ella Wilson. .

Debbie, the teller beside me, was gripping the edge of the counter, on tip-toe and aquiver with curiosity. I nudged her with my elbow. "What are we waiting for?" I whispered, and we joined the group.

Being barely five foot two, I couldn't see above the foursome already there. It was Joe who let me squeeze in front of him. Across the street flashing lights of two Caluga police cars bounced off Ballin's Drug Store windows. The murmur increased when three uniforms, half the town's police force, escorted a handcuffed man out the front door I stared in disbelief at the white-jacketed figure. His curly black haired head was bent, hiding a face so much like Sly Stallone's—*Jim. Oh my God*--I felt the blood draining from mine until I thought I'd faint.

"You okay?" Joe muttered in my ear.

I took a deep breath. Managed a weak smile as I struggled to get my heartbeat back on track. "Yeah, it's just—such a shock."

He gave me a funny look, but returned to the scene without another word. In a daze I watched a cop shove Jim into the back seat and slam the door. They'll be coming for me next, I thought. I unclenched my hands, desperate to hide the fear that swept through my body. It shook with relief when they drove away. The group slowly unwound, making comments I did not hear. It was an effort to pull myself together and return to Debbie's station.

"I can't believe Jim's been arrested." Debbie's green eyes shone with excitement. "I wonder what he could have done." She pushed a lock of red hair away from her freckled face. "Do you think he got into the drugs? Like, you know, sell 'em on the sly?"

"Yeah," Bud broke in. "That's where the big money is. Or maybe he just had his mitts in Ballin's till."

Both of them looked at me, waiting for an answer. Caluga is too small a town to keep a secret for long. They knew Jim and I had become an "item" shortly after he moved here, almost as soon as I did.

"I can't believe what happened either," I managed to mumble. Collecting the days transactions with shaking hands .I fled to the back room.

Bud's closing comment " Caluga hasn't had this much excitement since old man Lasky's bull got loose on Main Street," rang in my ears. I dumped the tapes onto my desk and collapsed in the chair behind it. He couldn't have known that he'd hit on the reason I'd soon be joining Jim behind bars.

I've lived in Caluga, Florida, population 4300 give or take one or two, all of my nineteen years. Maybe big enough when I was a little kid, but now? Every year since ninth grade, it got smaller and smaller, closing in, squeezing me until I think I'll end up a dried out husk. Until I met Jim. Who blew into town nine months ago, just when old Ballin needed a new pharmacist.

The image of our first meeting unrolled behind closed lids. The look his dark eyes gave me beneath thick black lashes. The eyebrows that made twin peaks above them. The strong nose in a lean, tanned face. He smelled like fresh air. *How could I have gotten into such a mess? How could I not?*

I forced myself to look around my "office" , a desk, chair and filing cabinet partitioned into a corner of the .employee's lounge. A shiny new computer on a stand that's the reason I'm here. Mr. Bacon, my boss, was a full-fledged accountant with years of experience. But I, fresh out of high school, was the only one young enough to know how to run it. Six months after I'd passed the tests, he retired. I doubt it was his choice.

You knew it couldn't last, I thought, sorting the papers into tidy piles. Remembering how jittery I'd felt at the beginning. Fear I'd be discovered. Guilt in knowing I was doing something wrong. All eventually overwhelmed by Jim's reassurances, my feelings for him.

Why was he arrested when it was me who'd committed the crime? Perspiration beaded my upper lip, made the papers stick to my hands. I wiped it away with a tissue but it kept coming back. It was no use. I had to get out of there. Decide what to do. Business would go on tomorrow as usual, no matter when the data was processed. Locking them into a file drawer, I picked up my purse and slipped out the back door.

After the air-conditioned bank July heat made me feel I was already walking into Hell. Late afternoon sun flared behind a row of rooftops. I could see a corner of the drugstore from the parking lot. A nervous tooth nibbled my lip I'll have to go over there. Maybe someone can tell me the charge that led to his arrest.

Ballin's is one of those old fashioned drug stores complete with soda fountain counter behind a row of stools. I'd

heard they were beginning to come back in style but this one is
.the real McCoy. Been in the same family for generations. With a
main street consisting of a dry goods store, barber shop, gas
station, a grocery, two bars and one stoplight, Caluga isn't
exactly a tourist resort. But one time I did overhear a couple of
outsiders raving about Ballin's "quaint charm" that reminded
them of the "good old days"

I passed a couple of boys in dirty shorts giggling over a
girlie magazine before the wooden rack Behind the soda
fountain, a skinny teen with a bad case of acne flirted with
the blonde perched before him. Sipping a root beer float. Maybe
given out "on the house"? I had more than one "freebie" from a
boy trying to make points, when I was her age.

The pharmacy at the rear of the store was in shadow. An
elderly woman, looking bewildered, was peering at a shelf of
OTC medications. Beside her Dorie Ballin held up a bottle of
cough medicine. "This should help until Jim gets back," she said.
"Then we can give you just what the doctor ordered.."

.   I caught her eye. Beneath her frizzy brown hair Dorie's
face looked harried. Transaction completed, and the woman out
of earshot, she turned to me. "Jim's been arrested,." she said.

"I know. I saw the cops taking him away,"

"Why? What has he done?"

I stared at her in surprise. Thick lens magnified grey-
green eyes. Circular rims accented the balloon shape of her face.

"That's what I was going to ask you. Didn't you hear anything? I mean one of the cops must have said something."

She shook her head. "I was in the back checking over some stock. I didn't even know they were here until I saw them taking him out the door."

We looked at each other. Our eyes mirrored a mutual mix of dismay, reproach and suspicion. Like half the women in town, single or otherwise, Dorie had a not-so-secret crush on one handsome James Maloney. And resented the fact that I was the one he chose. *Did she think she had first dibs on his affection? Because he showed up the same time illness forced her father to retire?*

After exchanging a half-hearted promise to tell the other if either of us heard any news, I left the store. By the time I reached my car, the heat had water dripping down my face. My blouse stuck to me in uncomfortable places. But what bothered me most was the question, should I go on home? How much longer would it be before Jim ratted me out? Maybe the cops were already at the house—the image of them being there, questioning my mom and dad grabbed at my stomach. I leaned against the car, swallowing the bile that rose in my throat.

Or does Jim really care enough for me to admit it was all his idea? To leave me out of it? *Come on—who're you kidding?* But hope overrode the mind's silent warning. I climbed into the car.

The cicadas were in shrill chorus when the house was in sight. The only vehicle in the driveway was Dad's old Ford pickup. I still pulled off the road onto the verge. A cloud of pinhead-size insects rose from the grass. No breeze stirred the leaves of the large live oak shading my Chevy. It was as if humid air was trapped between the tree and the ground.

I stared at the aging frame house , the faded yellow paint and wooden rocking chairs on the porch. Sometimes its walls wrapped around me like a blanket. More often lately, it was like being in a prison. No, a cell. It's the town that's the prison. The thought made me shiver. I had to get away. But where?

"You don't belong here," Jim had said. "Stuck out in the boonies, in this little burg the rest of your life." Describing some of the places he'd been, where we could go, drew me into his arms. Every time I hesitated, feeling bad about what I was doing, afraid of the consequences, he'd paint another picture. Too late now I realize it wasn't as an artist, but like a spider spinning a web. I shivered again, unconsciously pulling at the imagined strands.

We'd decided on Mexico. Not the exotic-sounding Acapulco that I wanted but some remote village with a name I never heard of, much less pronounce. "For a start," he'd assured me. "Only we need money. To break away. To follow our dream. Together."

The memory made me cringe. Even more at the word "money". There's $12 and some change in my purse. My one credit card was in a dresser drawer in my bedroom. In the house Like it or not I've got to take the chance. .

Mom met me at the front door, wearing a loose cotton dress. No doubt nice and comfortable in the summer, but it fit like a tent.. "Glad you're home," she said. "Ernie called. Just a few minutes ago."

"Oh?" Grabbing her lifeline, I lied "I'm supposed to be meeting him for dinner. He didn't leave a message?" At her "No," I said, "I'll get back to him in a minute. I gotta pee." and ran past her to my room.

What'd he want? I thought, leaning against the door I'd just shut. To tell me Jim was arrested? .By now the whole town must know. Mom hadn't said—but then I hadn't given her a chance. And if she thought I was now going out with Ernie, the man she wants me to marry…that would make her forget even that bit of news.

In my closet I yanked down a carry-on bag. Began to stuff it with jeans, shorts, tops—traveling clothes. But it didn't stop me from hearing her words. "Ernie'd make you a good husband," she'd said. "He's steady and honest. Hardworking. You can't get 'em any better than that." Maybe I'd even agreed. Dreams don't get very big in Caluga.

Until I met Jim and he whispered "Come live with me and be my love..." I never knew a man who recited poetry before. Or even read it. But I'll never forget how the words made me feel. Like floating on music. And all the sights I'd read about, places I never expected to be, were in reach.

"He's too old for you," Mom had said. OK, so Jim was close to 30. Big deal. Dad only muttered "I don't trust him worth a hoot," but couldn't—or wouldn't—tell my why. Was it because I was a girl, his only daughter? Must be the reason. That Jim was handsome, smart and had gone to college, wouldn't make any sense.

Only now Jim was in jail, and if I didn't get out of here fast, I'd be too. *How could I have done this to them?*

The question flooded the screen of my mind like a movie: I could see a cop standing in the room, speaking to my folks. Although I couldn't hear any words, I could imagine the expressions change on their faces. Confusion, disbelief, shame, anger and finally heart-wrenching grief scrolled past, each one leaving a knife in my chest. I sank to the floor on my knees, wishing I could die.

When that didn't happen I finally got to my feet. Stripped of emotion, I picked up my carry-on, and went to the window. Opening the screen I dropped the bag into the shrubbery. I almost followed it until I remembered my "date" with Ernie. Taking a deep breath, I opened my bedroom door.

The smell of baking powder biscuits, hot from the oven, filled the hall. No matter how steamy the day or cold the supper, there would be some kind of fresh-baked bread on the table. Crusty brown loaves, rolls, twisted or puffed, light fluffy biscuits or crumbly yellow cornbread. Growing up I'd help knead, punch and shape the dough. The memory lodged like a lump in my throat, making it hard to swallow.

Mom was piling biscuits in a basket. A platter of cold fried chicken, bowls of potato salad and three-bean salad were on the table. Already seated, Dad poured himself a glass of sweetened ice tea. Mom looked me over, one eyebrow raised on her flushed face.

"You going on a date like that?"

Whoops, I thought, looking down at the slacks and top I'd worn to work. Wilted and wrinkled now from the days heat. Naturally she'd expected me to change to a dress. Or at least something fresh and clean.

"We're only eating at Golden Corral,"

"He should be picking you up," Dad said, adding more sugar to his tea.

Like Jim? I forced a laugh. "It's Ernie, for heavens sake. I've only known him all my life."

He subsided with a mutter I couldn't make out. "Have a nice time," Mom said, as I started to leave. .I stopped. Turning, I threw an arm around her shoulder and gave her a hug. "I love you, mom" I half whispered, kissing her cheek. Then I fled.

The surprised look on her face, the grateful smile, followed me all the way out the front door. Tears ran down my face as I retrieved the bag, shoved it into the car, and drove away. Once out of sight of the house, I pulled off the road and wept like a lost child.

Finally reduced to gulps and sniffles, I looked around me. To my horror I found the emotional torture had only begun, for in a nearby yard I saw Mrs. Swanson. The frail, white-haired widow was watering her lawn. The hose she was holding in both arthritic hands could have been a sword, for all the pain that twisted my gut. To her I was the daughter she never had. She took care of me when my parents went out, fed me cookies, dressed my dolls in clothes she sewed. I called her "Nana", after my real grandma died. I loved her.

And to show my love, hers was one of the old people accounts I was bleeding into the dummy company Jim and I'd set up. In my name, of course. He'd insisted on that.

"Oh God, please help me," I begged aloud as the full weight of what I'd done fell on my head. I wanted to crawl under the dashboard. Instead I stepped on the gas and headed toward town. To turn myself in. Be arrested, go to jail like a common criminal was all I deserved. Because that's what I'd become.   .

I didn't even have nerve enough to do that. My head began to clear as I drove. *OK, the money's in my name. That means I might be able to give it all back before the cops take the computer. Only the bank's closed. But if I can't get in now, neither can they.*

By the time I neared the police station, my mind was made up. Overlooking the fact that all the cops had to do to get in, was go to the bank president, I drove right on by.

With no particular destination in mind, the sun was perched on the horizon before I realized I was in Mullet, a town not much bigger than Caluga. Along with a few more shops, there were two stoplights instead of one. I'd braked at the second when I remembered a former friend and neighbor lived there. Sally was older and moved away when she divorced, but we'd kept in touch.

To my relief, she was home. "Why Myra," Sally said when she opened the door. Blonde hair curled damply around her face. It looked as if she'd just stepped out of the shower and thrown on a flowered cotton robe. Bright blue eyes widened in surprise as she asked, "What brought you here? I mean, I didn't expect..."

"I know, I should have called. But—of course, if you're going out?"

"No, just trying to cool off. Come in, have a seat and tell me what's going on in Caluga."

The white wicker furniture cushioned in a tropical flower pattern in her living room, was typical Florida. I worried my lip, wondering how much to tell her. The two towns were only a few miles apart, but Jim's arrest only happened this morning. News didn't travel that fast. "Nothing much," I said. "I sorta needed to get away. For a little while."

"Trouble with your boyfriend? Your folks?"

"A little of both. They don't like him." Unwilling to spill the whole story, I said "Jim wants me to go away with him."

"And you don't know what to do."

I nodded. Sudden tears welled in my eyes and I turned away.

Her "Eaten yet?" was so unexpected, I almost looked up. "Neither have I," she said. "Stay here, while I put something together. Then we can talk. If you wish" and she disappeared into the kitchen.

I gazed out the double front window, half hearing a refrigerator door open, the clink of ice cubes, Sally humming to herself. Across the street a man stooped to pull up a clump of weeds on his way to his front door. For some reason I saw myself behind that door, and Ernie walking up the path. The longing to feel his strong arms around me , holding me close, was so real, I almost cried out.

We ate in an alcove off the kitchen. Fresh herbs lined the window sills. "You know," Sally said over the salad and iced tea,

"I knew Ernie but never met Jim. Your letters rave about him and how you're going to do all this traveling, but what's he really like? Why would a guy like him come to a town like Caluga?"

"I've told you how everyone thought it was a miracle. I mean Ballin didn't even have to look for his replacement. Jim was right there on his doorstep."

"How handy." I look up at the sarcastic edge to her voice, but her eyes are on her plate. She goes on, "Where did he come from to begin with?"

"I think he's from New York state. At least that's what a diploma has on it. " I stabbed at a tomato with my fork, trying to recall what little I knew of Jim's past. "And I know he was somewhere out west before he came to Caluga. Arizona, if I remember right."

The skeptical look in her eye made me squirm. "He said he was hoping to settle in a warm climate again. That's why he was looking around Florida."

"Is he divorced? Never married? What?"

My finger played with a fringe on the red placement while I recall how I kidded him about being so handsome, women were bound to fall all over him. And his unexpected reaction.

"You really don't know, do you." She didn't mean it as a question.

My face must have shown what I was feeling, for Sally changed the subject after that. Maybe she guessed I finally realized I'd been played for a fool. What she couldn't know was the price I still had to pay for being so blind to the game..

We were listening to the 10 o'clock news on Fox TV when I learned I was not alone. One of Jim's former loves— actually an ex-wife—had swallowed her pride and blown the whistle. In tracking him down, the police discovered he'd not only parted several women from their money, but was still married to two of them.

We stared at the screen with open mouths. "Boy," Sally breathed, "are you ever lucky"

If I wasn't trying to figure out how he could do all that by age 30, I would have said, you don't know the half of it.

***

Whatever conclusions Sally reached, I never knew for neither of us brought up his name again. The next morning I straightened out the plundered accounts. No one in the bank seemed to be aware of what had been going on under their very noses, and Jim wasn't talking.

The temptation to hold my tongue was so strong I could taste it. But the guilt I felt was even stronger. Just to live with myself, I'd have to tell the truth. I told Mr. Marsh what I'd done when I handed in my resignation.

Of course that opened the door to auditors, police and a judge. Somehow, maybe because I no longer worked in the bank, they managed to keep the whole affair out of the public eye. I was placed on a two year probation, but best of all. I have every reason to believe Mom and Dad never learned of my crime.

Me? I now wait tables in a restaurant large enough to have a cashier. The only money I handle, is what my customers leave me in tips.

12

A DAY AT THE BEACH

"Isn't anyone watching that child?" the old man demanded.

His angry eyes swept the beach. Save for a young couple huddled on a blanket, the spit of sand on the Gulf was deserted. He strode towards them, bare feet slapping noiselessly on the sand, flexing his knees a little to maintain his balance.

They lay face down, dozing in the early morning sun, while a small transistor beat out rock 'n roll above their heads. The girl wore a flowered bikini, so brief his anger reached the boiling point. He viciously jabbed her companion in the ribs with his big toe.

"Huh?" the youth grunted and lifted his head. The girl opened one eye

"Is that your child?"

"What?" They exchanged glances and the girl giggled.

"I said," the old man yelled, waving an arm in the general direction of the water, "is that your child? Out there."

The youth shifted his weight with a sigh. He leaned on one elbow and looked toward the Gulf. A small boy was riding the gentle swells on a gaily colored air mattress. "No," he said, and lay down again, eyes closed.

"He is out too far, Steve," the girl said. She sat upright, hands flat on the blanket and a breeze riffled the ends of her long, blonde hair. The old man could see that she was very pretty.

"For crying out loud, Ginny, I saw him. When I was his size I could swim like a fish." Her eyes caressed his lean, bronzed form as he muttered, "Besides, his Ma probably has him glued in her sights every minute."

A lot you know, the old man thought, remembering his daughters' occasionally desperate attempts to escape their numerous progeny.

The girl studied the length of her tanned legs, and wiggled her toes. "I'll keep an eye on him," she promised, but did not look up.

The old man bit off a "Thanks," and turned on his heel. What had he really expected? That they'd look at anyone but each other? Reaching the canvas chair he had set in the shade of a raggedy pine, he lowered his bony hips onto the seat.

"Irresponsible kids," he growled, and glared at them. They lay quietly, the youth's arm intimately draped over the girl's back. Snorting in disgust, he fumbled for his pipe. He filled it from a battered pouch, his pale blue eyes fastened on the child.

The boy paddled idly, curly dark head inches from the water as he peered over the edge of the float. He's a scrawny runt, the old man thought, and white as a sheet. Must be a tourist.

He lit his pipe, protecting the flame with a gnarled hand, thinking it sure looks peaceful. The sea was almost flat, a white-flecked, translucent green that whispered across the open shallows to curl over the shore. Gulls wheeled against the sky, their cries cutting through the stillness. He stretched his legs to the mottled sun, wondering what he was worried about. It was going to be a good day, no reason to get upset. The child was not his problem, anyway.

He yawned, musing no more responsibilities. No more sweating out the old rat race. No more reason to—the old man straightened abruptly. The unfinished thought nibbled at his mind. He pushed it away, aware of the ending, aware of the danger of knowing. He and Edith did a good job, he told himself. Son a doctor, girls all married to successful men. He nodded, but his eyes were bleak. *Maybe there'll be a letter today.*

Suppressing the hope, he glanced at the boy. "My God, that child looks like Timmy." The knife of memory stabbed him and his lip curled in pain. A speeding car, the broken body, his daughter Mary's grief and terrible guilt , 'I couldn't watch him every minute!'. And even as he comforted her, his own unspoken, unreasonable question. *Why not?*

So long ago. The spasm quieted to a dull ache. One grandchild out of how many—10 -11? He struggled through the jumble of half-forgotten names and faces, trying to recall when he had last seen even one of them. *Becky. She had stopped by when on her honeymoon.* Two-three years ago. Good Lord, he thought, I am a great-grandpa now. He sank helplessly into the chair.

The old man stared down at his shrunken body. The leather-colored skin clung to the stringy muscles of arms and legs, barely covering the bony protuberances. If anything happened, what could he do? Shaking his head, he cast a worried glance at the boy. The child lay quietly, head pillowed on his arms, drifting—the old man leaned forward, body tense. The tide was running out.

He rose to his feet, took two hesitant steps, then turned and walked towards the couple. The youth was on his knees, dribbling sand onto the girl's back. She said, "Cut that out," and gave him a shove. He fell backwards, landing at the old man's feet.

The youth flashed him a broad grin. "Sorry about that," he said.

The old man frowned. "I need your help."

"What for?"

"That child on the float. The tide's turned."

"So?"

But the girl had jumped to her feet. She swept the hair from her eyes. "He's right, Steve," she said.

"So now the kid can walk in."

The old man's voice grew testy. "There's a channel out there."

"And a sandbar on the other side."

"Steve…" the girl said.

"Okay. Okay." He hoisted himself up with careful deliberation, and brushed the sand from his body. He ambled toward the water, the old man and the girl trailing behind him. At the edge he stopped. Cupping his hands around his mouth he yelled, "Hey, kid.. Kid! Come on in."

The child did not stir. "He must be asleep," Ginny said. She looked expectantly at Steve

"Well, what do you want me to do? Go out there and tow him in?"

"Yes."

"And have his folks jump on me for spoiling his fun? Don't be ridic." He jerked a thumb toward a nearby jetty. "What do you want to bet they're on the next beach."

"And if they're not?"

"Oh, for Pete's sake. You know as well as I do that the current will carry him back into shore further down. Besides, no one in their right mind would let a kid like that out alone in the water, if he couldn't swim." He turned his back on them.

Ginny looked doubtful. "I guess he's right," she said to the old man. "Steve knows the Gulf pretty well—this part, anyway. He's lived here most of his life." She gave him a hesitant, apologetic smile and walked away. "He'll be all right," she called over her shoulder.

The old man looked down at the water. Minute waves hissed and foamed, he could see sand particles suspended in them as they broke over his feet. Feeling a little foolish, he began to make his way toward the child. You're an idiot, he thought, as the sea climbed his legs. What could possibly happen on a day like this?

He stopped, hands on hips, noting the deepening blue that marked the channel. The distance between himself and the child, vaguely conscious of a growing rush of sound. He turned his head. A motorboat was coming wide open, throwing twin sheets of spray, down the middle of the channel.

"Boy! Look out!"

His shriek lost itself in the roar of the engine, and he hurriedly began to swim, his eyes glued to the float. He saw the boy lift his head, the boat quickly swerve. Saw the bright green and white stripes of the float, caught by the backwash, rise in the air, flipping the child into the Gulf, coming to rest again beyond reach. He saw the boy go under, then pop to the surface, hands clawing at the water, his mouth wide open in surprise. The boy flailed the water with his arms, his eyes round in panic, and the old man doubled his efforts. He had been a strong swimmer once, but the years had worn him down. He labored frantically, gasping for breath

The boy grabbed at him. Sharp nails raked his face, a finger poked him in one eye. A foot kicked him in the stomach and he doubled up, unable to breathe The water closed over his head, a silky green, and he tried to push the boy away. The child clung to him with wiry tentacles of arms and legs, forcing him down…

Someone was strangling him. He struggled against the grip, tried to raise his hands—

"Hold still," The voice came from far away.

The old man opened his eyes. Floating above him was the blurred face of the boy. There seemed to be a weight on his chest. Evidently the child was astride him. Water lapped about his ears, left salt in his mouth. Someone was holding his head above the waves. He could hear short, labored grunts, sense movement beneath his body. He relaxed, giving himself to the cradle of the sea.

A jolt jarred him to consciousness. The old man found himself sitting on the sandy bottom, his head, bent and dripping, between his flexed knees. There was motion, voices around him, but he did not look up. The sun warmed him, played on the tiny bits of shell that ebbed and swirled about his hips.

A hand gripped his shoulder. "You all right?"

The old man raised his head. It was Steve. His brown hair wet, and tanned body shining golden in the sun. He gave a weak nod. The youth squatted beside him.

"Where's the boy?" the old man finally asked.

"Ginny took him home. She's going to tell his folks where to head in." A grin flickered across his face, than vanished. There was an embarrassed silence. He blurted, "You're quite a guy."

The old man gave him a startled look. Steve's gray eyes were anxious, respectful, oddly vulnerable. And you had to save us both, he thought bitterly. He turned away. "I did what I had to do," he said. "And so did you."

Steve drove a finger into the sand. "Yeah," he muttered.

The heroic deed spoiled by human frailty? What can I say? the old man thought. That we rarely live up to our own image? That a lifetime of learning this does not ease the sting? His mouth twitched in silent laughter. He said, "That's the important thing, isn't it? Even for an old man."

"I guess so," Steve said. His trailing fingers captured a small shell and he held it up. It was a delicate, perfectly formed scallop. He studied it. Then, rising to his feet, he drew back an arm and in one easy motion, flipped the shell far into the Gulf

He turned. "I hope I'm half the man you are," he said, "when I'm your age."

The old man watched him walk away, feeling pleasure diffuse his aching body. He saw Ginny run to meet him, long hair streaming behind her. They're really not bad kids, he thought, as hand in hand, they clambered over the jetty. A wry smile pulled at his lips, when he said aloud, "I can even forgive them for being young."

St. Anthony Messenger, Summer, 1970.

13

THE CLOSE OF DAY

It is September and in Pennsylvania, where I come from, the first frost sets fire to the mountains. But I'm in Tampa, Florida and the heat of the summer has not yet released its merciless grip on the city. I sit in my car, patting the sweat off my face with a tissue as I watch Lucinda Simmons crab her way down the uneven walk.

"That woman has two Pekinese running around loose," she says, opening the passenger door with a wrinkled hand. The fingernails are rimmed with dirt.

"She had the nerve to tell me I'd have to keep my dogs on a leash."

The aggrieved tone of her voice prickles beneath my skin. "That's the city law, Mrs. Simmons."

"Bosh. Then why doesn't she follow it?" Her snow-white hair is half covered with a dingy straw hat. She ducks her head, pulls her right leg into the Toyota with a grunt. "Trouble," she complains, "ever since I fell. Right on the driveway, and then blood poisoning."

It is a litany I'm beginning to know by heart. How could she possibly remind me of my mother-in-law?

"You'd think with two dogs she'd have a fenced-in yard."

"The last place did."

"It was awful. You could see that. Out in the middle of nowhere. No stores. You know I need to be on a bus line—"

And, I silently finish for her, have two bedrooms in a decent neighborhood with a landlord who allows pets. Like a dozen cats and two dogs. When I had picked her up this morning, a yippy terrier left a trail of nervous puddles across the bare floor. The place smelled so bad I could barely keep from gagging.

Ellen, my mother-in-law loves animals too. She has a Siamese cat, Chin, and a poodle named Gigi. When she travels, which is often, she leaves them with us. But there's no comparison...

"You don't have much time left," I say, struggling to hide a mounting resentment. It is now 4:30 and, except for a brief stop at a drive-through for lunch, I've carted her around since 9 o'clock. "I was told your lease is up in two days."

"He doesn't dare put me out in the street." Two wiry hairs on her chin quiver in indignation.

That's not what Mark told me, I think. For some reason my 11 year old son and Mrs. Simmons had bonded shortly after we moved onto her street almost two years ago. In fact, my youngest child is the reason why I'm helping her chase after her increasingly impossible dream. How could I refuse to aid a poor old lady facing eviction? "Where next?" I ask with a resigned sigh.

Eyes faded to a colorless smoke peer at a piece of paper through thick trifocals. "Williamston, I think." She shoves it under my nose. "Maybe you can make it out. I can hardly see anything with these specs." Fingers adjust the frame and she nods. "Once I get settled, I can get a job. Buy a new pair."

A job? I eye her stooped and shrunken figure in disbelief. She must be in her eighties!

Ellen just turned 65. Her trim body passes for half that age, and her facial structure is just beginning to soften. Although now a widow, she hasn't worked a day in her life.

A spasm of guilt reminds me, neither do I. At least not since we moved to Florida. "I volunteer at Tampa General—" did I actually say that out loud?

"I took care of an old lady for awhile," Mrs Simmons says, ignoring me. "Fixed her lunches, did some laundry, nothing heavy. But after a month the daughter came back and didn't need me anymore."

She falls quiet, sucks on her dentures. All of a sudden she says, "Ben went of a bad heart. Died in my arms. We hadn't lived in Florida six months." Her voice is a mix of regret and accusation. "Trouble. Nothing but trouble ever since."

For some reason I see Ellen falling and breaking her hip. It had happened last year, a freak accident over the holidays. She could have afforded a private nurse, once she was out of the hospital, but Bill is her only child and I was home She was with us for eight weeks. I turn into Williamston.

"Ben used to play the piano while I sang," Mrs. Simmons says. "Didn't know I was a concert singer, did you." It isn't a question. She breaks into a tremulous, off-key song from *Naughty Marietta*. It sounds like nails on a blackboard. Her fingers pluck at a flower-shaped cluster pinned on her drooping chest. One of the stones is missing.

"I got this pin for one program," she says. "Eastern Star. I have some lovely jewelry , very valuable. And gowns. I used to teach voice, too, you know.I was really in demand." Her explosive cackle splits the silence. "Who would want an old lady to sing for them now?"

Her words give an unexpected tug to my heart. Rekindled the sense of loss I feel when I think of the dance lessons I took to reach a dream—modern, ballet, tap, jazz—only to watch it blow away like so much fairy dust. "At least you had your 15 minutes," I mutter under my breath.

We reach our destination. The small house is set back from the street. What is visible above a tall, densely floral skirt of plants, needs a coat of paint. Mrs. Simmons hoists herself from the seat to begin her slow, reluctant journey up the front walk.

From where I sit, I can see a small general store on the corner. A green painted bench marks a bus stop. The neighborhood is so quiet, I wonder if it's filled with retirees. The house even has a fenced-in back yard—I spot a portion of it sagging behind an untrimmed hibiscus. All the requirements. For the first time in this long day I have a glimmer of hope.

One look at her face on her return, is enough to kill it

"It only has one bedroom," she says.

"But Mrs. Simmons, there's only one of you."

"Where can I put company?"

It is too much. "You have a couch," I snap. She does have one, doesn't she? I try to picture what I saw in that houseful of animals, when I picked her up. Not much, I think, maybe a couple of chairs, but I really didn't go inside...

"I do need one," she admits. "And drapes. My rugs are at the cleaners. It'll be good to get a nice place where I'm not ashamed to have company. Like it used to be."

"Then you'll take this one."

She looks at me as if seeing me for the first time. "Of course not," she says. "Ben and I had a lovely home with marble floors, a formal garden. The music room had French doors that opened on to a lawn. It stretched all the way to the river. We had—"

My eyes are drilling furious holes into her head as she rambles on. She is senile, I think. She must be. Why didn't I see it before? Defeated, I start the engine and turn towards home. It is an effort to keep from pressing the pedal to the floorboard.

There is nothing wrong with Ellen's mind, yet without warning the image of her in my house with her broken hip, pops up. Once again I hear the querulous demands, see her expression of martyrdom, watch the way she clings to Bill. I squirm with guilt as I recall my resentment. Of her, for disrupting my life, of Bill for being gone all day, of the kids, who silently accused me of being short with Nana, when they were rarely home to help.

Ellen. Mrs. Simmons. There's no comparison. Almost frantic, I shove the images and what they construed, into the depths of my mind. I love my mother-in-law, I tell myself, admire her lifestyle, hope to be like her when I reach her age.

"You have a good boy," Mrs. Simmons says.

I start. "Yes. Mark is a sweetheart," I agree. "You have children?"

"Three. And five grandchildren." She looks out the window. "I never see them anymore."

Mark had told me they all live far away. I'm glad we've reached her house, for I don't know what to say.

A large orange cat rises from the sagging wicker chair on the front stoop. Stretches and curls back into a ball. Mrs. Simmons looks at it with vacant eyes. I open her door, help her make an arthritic exit. I turn to go. She asks, "You'll be back tomorrow?"

I look at the ground, fighting back the urge to say "No". The sidewalk beneath our feet is cracked, broken at the edges. I take a deep breath. "Yes," I say, "if you agree to take the house on Williamston, providing the last two houses on your list are unsuitable."

For a moment, a defiant spark lights her pale eyes, and as quickly fades. "It was a fairly nice place at that," she admits. "Maybe we can forget about the others. I'll see."

With a gracious nod of dismissal, Mrs. Simmons straightens up to walk, proud and erect, to her front door.

14

THE HONEYMOON SUITE

"They reserved the honeymoon suite about a month or so ago, don't remember exact, 'cept I recall his voice sounded pretty shaky. Course I just put that down to weddin' jitters.

"Actually it ain't a "suite" at all. Just a room with big windows and a couple of comfy chairs to sit in. We lay out some books to go along with the Bible, and there's an ironstone pitcher filled with flowers. My favorites are those fat peonies, they look so pretty against the white. And it's got its own bathroom—well, you saw it. Anyways, I never guessed...

"Oh. My name is Ada Lankowski now—that's L-a-n-k-o-w-s-k-i---married Ben about two years ago. He's a good man, good with tools. Anymore it's gotten so hard to get a handyman I just figured it was easier to marry one.

"The inn's real old. Built around the time of the Revolutionary War—don't know if Washington ever slept here but he could've. Ever since Fred, he's my second husband, passed on it's been harder and harder to keep it up. Not that I get many customers anymore. Niagara Falls don't seem to be as popular as it once was. We keep hopin' the new casino will liven things up a bit, maybe get the tourists comin' over from Canada, but…

"The Blackstones? Oh yes. Well, I couldn't believe it. When they finally got here my mouth hung open like it was catchin' flies. So's would yours if you'd been in my shoes. I mean here I was waitin' for some young buck and his girl when in comes this little ole lady with white hair and glasses and a little ole man hardly bigger round than she was. 80-85 years old if they were a day. You know they say if you live together long enough you sorta start lookin' like each other? Well, they sure did. And they wanted the honeymoon suite? What for? I mean they was OLD.

"Well, I finally got my mouth back where it belonged, and I asked 'em if they was just married, sorta kiddin' you know? Not that it ain't possible, 'specially nowadays, what with Viagra and all but…Anyways the old guy looks up from signin' the register and smilin' at her just as sweet as you please, says "In a way.". She don't say nothin', just looks sorta confused, but he gives her a hug and tells me, "I promised her when we wed I'd see she'd get a real honeymoon someday. It's taken me fifty years but, by gum, I finally did it.".

"You can see he's pretty proud of hisself and I'm feelin' pretty good about it myself. I mean how many men do somethin' like that? After fifty years it's a wonder you can even get 'em to talk to you. Anyways, Ben took their bag, got 'em settled in their room—no, I didn't think it odd they only brought one bag. They were just stayin' a few days, and old people don't need much clothes…In fact, Callie says what they was wearin' musta been a good 20-30 years outa date.

"Who's Callie? She's the high school girl I have part time. You already talked to her—Elizabeth Ann Moore? That's her real name. She likes to be called Callie 'cause she was born in California, or some dumb reason like that, and the nickname stuck. Lovely girl, smart as a whip. Plannin' on going to college and I bet she could get one of them scholarships, no trouble at all.

"You know she thinks you're pretty cute. What made you take up police work? I bet you're wife ain't too happy—oh, you ain't married. I see. Wait'll I tell…Okay, okay. So we was talkin' about the Blackstones. You needn't get huffy about it.

"We didn't see 'em much, they pretty well stuck to their room when they weren't walkin' somewheres. No, they didn't have a car. Got here in a taxi and took one when they went to the Falls. They liked to walk in the garden—he always seemed to be holdng her hand wherever they went. I got some nice flowers, 'specially the roses. They're in full bloom now. Would you like to see em? Then how about a cup of tea? No? Mind if I make myself a cup? Thanks. All this is such a strain…

"Now where was I? I really can't tell you much about 'em. Don't recall her even saying "good morning" or "thank you", but Mr. Blackstone did come into the kitchen yesterday— why that was their 50th anniversary. Just before they went to the Falls. Sat right where you are. I'd baked cookies and he ate a couple and had some tea while he talked with Ben and me.

"That's when we learned they'd had a small farm on Long Island. Never made any money until he sold it to some developer. For a lot less than its worth, I bet. He told us he and Dot—that's his wife—grew up together, always knew they'd get married and have a big family. But they only had one kid, a son, and when they lost him in the Vietnam War, she never got over it. Said she'd been going downhill ever since. But that's all I know.

"Callie thinks it likely she had Alzheimers and maybe he couldn't take care of her anymore. To tell the truth he didn't look like he was in the best of health hisself. Anyways, the only time I remember hearing her speak was when they got back from the

Falls. She looked so happy, even if what she said didn't make much sense. What do I mean? Just before they went up to their room, she smiled at him and said, clear as you please, "I'm ready now."

"We found 'em the next day. Today. I'm all mixed up, it was just before I called. You oughta know. You've been here ever since.

"No, like I've been tellin' you they stuck close to their room. We only serve breakfast and they usually ate it up there. Your appetite sorta falls off when you're old so when I didn't hear from them this morning, I paid it no mind. I was also expectin' my church ladies over—I'm Methodist and twice a month we have dessert and coffee or tea before…

"You already know it was Callie who found 'em. She comes in after school like I said, and by then the ladies had left. I was cleanin' up so I sent her upstairs to see if the Blackstones were in and wanted anythin' and then I heard her scream…it made the hair rise right up on the back of my neck, I can tell you.

"Ben was sittin' here in the kitchen with me and we both run up the stairs as fast as we could, but one look and we knew there was nothin' we could do. They was lyin' there just as you saw 'em, her in a pretty white nightgown, him bare-chested, lookin' as if they'd just fallen asleep. Holdin' hands.

"Think you'll find some kind of poison when you took that bottle of champagne? No, I don't know where—where—or when they got it. As I've said they liked to walk and some stores ain't far from here. You know, what I can't get over is how the ole guy had everything all planned out so nice and tidy. I mean he left money to pay for the room, even a real nice tip for Callie, on the table. The funeral is all taken care of, what to do with their things—they didn't have any family left, so...

"Of course I read the note. What do you mean, did I disturb anything? It ain't a crime scene. Is it?

"You say he killed her? Come on—what difference does that make. She *knew*. Why spoil it? Don't the good book say 'To love and to cherish 'til death do us part'? In all the years I've run this inn, the honeymooners I've seen come and go, they're the first ones who really knew what those words meant. To turn their wish to *never* part, into a murder-suicide—Why can't you people just let it be?"